Love Unapologetic
The Frederick
Family Series

ISBN-13: 9781234567890

ISBN-10: 1477123456

Cover design by: Art Painter

Library of Congress Control Number: 2018675309

Printed in the United States of America

Contents

Trigger Warnings

Ok baby love this trigger warnings page is about to get long and some may send you running but understand that is ok, please do what is best for you. Now let's get to good and gritty.

- Explicit language
- Graphic sex scenes
- Various sex kink/fetish content
- Mild stalking
- Kidnapping
- Graphic violence
- Pregnancy
- Drug use
- Poly relationships
- Orgies (Multiple sex partners at once)
- Suicide attempt
- Child abuse (conversion camp)
- Cheating (Not main characters)
- Extreme Christians
- Forced Medical Procedure
- Child abandonment
- Abortion

Yoruba Translations

1. Brother – Arakunrin
2. Mama – Iya
3. Son – Omo
4. Daughter – Omobinrin
5. My Love – Ife mi
6. Fuck – Fokii
7. Bitch – Bishi
8. Daddy – Baba
9. This stupid bitch – Bishi omugo yii
10. Sinful Sanctuary – Ila mimo else
11. My safe place – Ibi aabo mi

Family Tree

The Fredericks Family

Matriarch: Valerie Fredericks

Sons:

- **Montavius Fredericks** – Married to La'Meira Jennings
- **Jax Fredericks** – In a relationship with La'Meira Jennings
- **Dean Fredericks** – Married to Kelia
- **Chase Fredericks** – Engaged to Kenya
- **Marshall Fredericks** – Married to Bree
- **Demetrius Fredericks**

Adopted Brothers

- Blake Rue – Also known as Money
- Tru Valentine

Montavius, Jax & La'Meira's Children:

- Mariah
- Za'Meir
- Za'Mara
- Jackson
- Montavius Jr.

- Ayomi

Dean & Kelia's Children:

- Denise
- Myla
- Darius
- Mercy
- Delia

The Jennings Family

Matriarch: Lorraine Jennings

Daughter:

- **La'Meira Jennings** – Wife to Montavius, partner to Jax

Brother:

- **Tone Jennings**

Prologue

Dean and Kelia Fredericks are no strangers to chaos, but marriage has brought them calm and a happy routine they never knew they craved. Tucked away in the Alabama countryside, they've created a beautiful life— raising their newborn daughter, Delia, alongside their four adopted children with fierce love and intentionality. Their connection is deep, raw, and intensely passionate. But the peace they've built is tested when both sides of their families come together for the first time over what was supposed to be a simple dinner.

What begins with polite smiles and tense introductions quickly spirals when Kelia's sister keeps trying to drop hints about her new families lifestyle and once it is discovered a comment is dropped that cuts too deep. Suddenly, her childhood trauma is laid bare, forcing her to confront the darkest parts of her past in front of people who don't know the full story—and some who never cared to. For years, Kelia's silence was her shield, but now, she's tired of shrinking. This time, she's ready to own every piece of herself, including the parts of her sexual identity and experience that were once laced with pain and shame.

As Kelia steps fully into her truth, the Fredericks family faces a storm of its own. Enemies from their past have returned, carrying old grudges and new weapons, determined to dismantle everything the family has built.

Their compound, once a haven, becomes a battleground for loyalty, protection, and survival.

But Dean and Kelia aren't backing down. Not from the whispers, not from the threats, and certainly not from the love that's carried them through every twist and turn. Together, they must balance healing with action, vulnerability with strength, and parenting with partnership.

In the midst of it all, they rediscover what it means to love loudly, live freely, and stand in their truth—even when the world demands they apologize for it. **Love Unapologetic** is a story of growth, resilience, and the kind of love that doesn't flinch in the face of fire.

Chapter 1

Dean Fredericks

"Um good sir where are you going with my baby." Kelia questioned me as she walked into our daughter Delia Meira Fredericks room as I am getting her dressed.

"Babe it's time she joins the triplets at the main house baby room. I won't have you over working yourself woman. Today will be your first me day enjoy it." I inform her as pick our three-month beauty up. We started calling Meira, Montavius, and Jax house the main house since we all tend to gather there. Also since only their home and ours have been finished everyone else stays there.

"But I don't wanna and before you say it no, I'm not going."

"Babe it's been four months even I'm going back to the house." She just rolls her eyes gives Delia a kiss then me and leaves the room. I have been worried about her possibly having postpartum depression. She's become very withdrawn, moody is a damn understatement, amongst other things so I decided before we go that route and get her a therapist, I'll give her some me time since she truly could just be overwhelmed with all the shit we've had to deal with lately. I grab her baby bag and head over to the house but by the time I make it to the baby room that has the three nannies we hired I am getting a text from the security guard at the gate.

"Bro did you get the text too?" Jax questions me as he walks up with baby Jackson and Ayomi then Monty comes around the corner holding Mj. My brothers look so exhausted and sad to be honest. I don't think any of us have really slept well and it has nothing to do with all the babies we have in our lives now.

"Yea what the hell is CPS doing at our damn gate?" I respond after handing Delia over to the nanny name Bado, she recently moved here from India but came highly recommend from the agency we hired all the nannies from due to her being a licensed pediatric nurse and child psychology degree. Jax hands Jackson and Ayomi to nanny Trisha then Monty hands Mj over to Chance the only male nanny we decided to hire.

"I don't know what the fuck they want but they might as well leave before I get in more of a bad mood than I am already in." Monty has that look in his eyes that lets me know we might be getting rid of some bodies today if people don't steer clear of him. Since it's not time for most of to head out we hop on one of the golf carts and head to the front gate. We decided to gate the entire property with a titanium six-foot-tall fence, that damn thing took the builders over eight months to finish. We hop off the golf cart once we make it to the security gate shelter.

"You check their ID's." Monty questions when we walk up to the gate guard and he responds with handing them over to him. He scans them with his phone while I pull them up in the CPS agents directory and sure enough, they are real employees. I tap Monty on the shoulder to let him know then the gate starts to slide back revealing the two agents.

"What do you want?" Monty asks in a gruff and snipped tone. That man is truly not in the mood, and I think it's best I take over with them.

"Good morning, sir, we are here due to a report of child neglect for the child Za'Meir Fredericks?" The tall blond woman who looks like she needed to stop missing meals before her scrawny ass disappears says.

"Well, I'm his father and these are his uncles. He is sitting happily at our dining room table enjoying breakfast with his sisters and cousins which you just took us away from so if you would leave our property before you annoy me any further, I'd greatly appreciate it." Monty explains and then gives the signal for the guard to close the gate after he hands them back their ID's. He turns to walk away and so did we until this stupid bitch and whoever the quiet scared looking white boy with her runs around the gate shouting.

"Mr. Fredericks we will be the judge of him being fine and if you try that again I will gladly come back with the police." This bitch has balls. I wonder how long she would last in target practice.

"You must not like your life very much stepping around my gate. You are on my property and interrupting breakfast with my family-"

"Arakunrin let me deal with her just go back to the family. Jax take him please." I instruct him and he grabs Monty by the arm trying to get him to go to the cart. He gives in after Jax whispers something in his ear when looking at his phone.

"Ok Ms. Fields look there is no need for you to be here. You received a report about one child out of eleven that live on this property so clearly whomever made said report is targeting him. Our lawyer is speaking with your supervisor Mr. Burke as we speak and I'm sure your phone will be ringing soon." I let the guard know to watch her leave as I head back to the other golf cart for when we have guest. I hear her phone start to ring as she's walking back to her vehicle. This morning is already starting out with bullshit and I hope the rest of the day goes better. Before I get back to the house Monty is texting me the info of who filed the report and it looks like I'll get to blow off some steam at the range.

Chapter Two

Kelia Fredericks

Dean is working on my nerves with this main house shit and taking my baby. I don't want a free day I want my mini-Meira. I really need Meira herself. I can't believe three months ago she almost left us for good and she hasn't been the same since. Hell I haven't been the same. Between almost losing her and having Delia my brain hasn't had a break. I don't feel like myself mentally or physically, nothing fits right. Dean doesn't think I know but I know he plans on getting me a therapist. I think I may need one but I'll try something else first. I decide to take advantage of my Me day and get dressed. Thankfully the men left about an hour ago so I don't have to worry about dealing with them. Heading out the front door to the infamous main house. I walk right in after tapping my watch on the lock pad to unlock the door. I swear these men took the security of our homes to a whole other level. I take the back way up to where I'm going then enter through the entrance in the closet. When I come into the room she's laying on the bed looking like the angel she is. I get into the bed with her, rubbing my chin on her shoulder to see if she will finally respond.

"Hi baby mama." La'Meira greets me rubbing my hand that I wrapped around her waist as we spoon.

"Morning love. I missed you. How are you feeling today?" I express kissing her on the shoulder.

"I know, I miss you too. Today is better. I got up and showered with Monty but I still wouldn't let him touch me." She says turning over on her back. I lay my head on her chest and she starts running her hands through my hair.

"When are you going to stop punishing them two anyways? The family hasn't been the same." I ask and this is just what I needed.

"You think I'm over doing it?"

"Only you can say that babe." I feel like they were out of line with the decision they made but I also get why they did make it.

"I just can't believe they made the decision for me on whether I can have another baby for God sakes." I can tell she's getting emotional, but I think she needs to let it out.

"I get that I do. The only thing is I get why they made it though." She jumps up at that comment to turn and look at me.

"Seriously Kelia they had that woman remove my damn uterus without talking to me about it first."

"Wait a minute now you were talking to her about tying your tubes and they only did it because you were bleeding to fucking death Meira. We all thought we lost you." She starts tearing up then staring ahead and then I notice Monty, Jax, and Dean are all standing at the bedroom door watching us. Jax sits on the edge of the bed while Monty kneels on the floor on her side of the bed as Dean crawls in behind me.

"I see you finally came out the house." He whispers in my ear and I just nod.

"Ife mi we never wanted to take your choice away from you. You have to know that but I literally almost died looking at you bleeding to death on that bed."

"We did the only thing we could to save your life my Phoenix. She couldn't find the source of the bleed. I couldn't, we couldn't lose you. It's been like living with only a small part of my heart still functioning with you not speaking to us." Jax expresses rubbing her leg that's under the blanket.

"Not being able to touch you, not even a hug has literally shattered my heart into pieces Ife mi." Monty expresses next and you would never think these big ass men would be crying like they are, even Dean has tears in his eyes. She hasn't been talking to him either since he agreed with the decision they made.

"We aren't trying to guilt you into understanding Lil Dove. We just want you to see things from our point of view. I almost lost my brother and best friend that day. Monty literally fought to stay by your side while having a heart attack after your flat lined for the second time.

That day almost tore the entire family apart and that was the only thing they could do. We all felt helpless." Dean pours out his heart and I turn to wrap him in my arms because I know how hard that day was for him. When we all noticed that Monty was literally fighting a heart attack and in so much pain he fell to his knees holding his arm. The first person to notice it was more than him being sick over what was happening with La'Meira was Jax and it made sense with how close they are. The doctors tried to make everyone leave the room and for him to get help but that man would not budge. Jax made them bring another bed inside the room after the decision was made to do her hysterectomy and to work on him. Thankfully the medicine they gave him worked as it was mild but it could have been so much worse. La'Meira finally caves and pulls Monty into her arms squeezing him tight as the realization that she could have actually lost him as well.

"Ok I'm sorry for being stubborn for so long. Ughh it's not like I wanted more kids anyway. Can you guys forgive me?" She asks turning to look at each of us. Monty simply gives her a heated kiss then lays his head on her chest and so does Jax once he crawls in between her legs then lays his head on her stomach. I give her a kiss on the cheek laying my head on her other shoulder then Dean gives her a kiss then moves to lay between my legs his head on my chest and I just rub my hands over his waves.

"Ife mi I'm going to fuck the shit out of you if you keep rubbing my neck like that." Monty declares and my clit jumps at the thought of us all possibly having sex, which is crazy because I haven't wanted sex in months.

"Do what you gotta do Big Daddy." Before I can wrap my head around what is happening Jax is hopping out the bed to walk over to the door that leads to our Sinful Sanctuary that's connected to their master bedroom, Monty stands snatching Meira out of the bed on one smooth movement throwing her over his shoulder, and Dean grabs me out of nowhere and doing the same. When we get in the room Monty and Jax are already undressing Meira, she has actually been wearing clothes since she has not spoken to them. The room screams sex with the emerald green walls, soft lights, California king size bed in the middle of the room, covered in silk black sheets, plush black carpet, dark cherry wood cabinets with glass doors lining half of the left wall that showcases all the different types of sex toys, on that same wall hangs two swings that face each other, an Andrews cross on the right wall, and next to that the infamous bench from their honeymoon. Now when you walk in on either side of the door there are large navy-blue armchairs if you just wanted to watch or whatever comes to mind.

"Hmm you wanted to try the bench right my sweetness?" I nod my head as I am so turned on and I guess I just needed to start the process of healing our family for it to happen.

"Now you know you are to use your word Sweetness." Oh, shit he's in play mode.

"Yes, I want to try the bench, Ghost." I say low and seductive.

"Strip." He commands and I do as he demands. While stripping down to my birthday suit, I hear moaning from our left. Jax and Monty have Meira in one of the swings with Monty on his knees his face planted nose deep in her pussy while Jax is fucking her throat as she leans back in the swing.

"We will get with them in a bit, you get over." He directs gently pushing me forward into position. He straps my ankles with the thick black velvet soft restraints as I lean over the bar in the middle and then he comes around to strap in my wrist. He walks over to one of the cabinets and opens a drawer to pull out this long black leather flogger. When he walks past Meira and the guys he rubs it across her shoulder then her stomach making her moan even more around Jax's dick. At the same time she squirts all over Monty's beard and he clamps down on her clit swallowing every drop. Dean walks over to me with a wicked grin on his face and I know I am in for the time of my life. At first he just tickles me from my neck down to my ass with the talon parts of the flogger then in a snap of his wrist he sends the talons smacking across my ass in a rapid succession of three hits followed by it slowly dragging across my soft skin. I understand now why Meira was so damn turned on when they did this to her last year, this shit may hurt but for some damn reason it feels so fucking good at the same time. I feel the tingle starting at my toes shooting up through my legs right to my pussy inciting my everlasting ache for my man's dick or tongue.

"Fuucckk." I moan when he takes the flogger and slapping my fully exposed pussy with it. I feel a gush of liquid from my love box then his warm tongue lapping up every drop moaning as he does.

"Damn you have always been my favorite desert baby." He groans as he flattens his tongue licking from my clit then dipping his tongue in my honeypot swirling it around to like up all my juices. That man since the day we met at the club has savored every part of my body during sex. My brain flashes back to our first night together, I had been attending the club for about two or three weeks but still hadn't played with one. Now that I think about it I'm sure he was watching me the whole time. I watched and played with myself only until he finally decided to walk up on me one night during their masquerade party wearing his Ghostface mask and something about his voice plus the commanding but sensual energy coming off him in waves made me go with him that night. I have been happy with that decision ever since then.

"Mhmm shit D... Deeaann." I moan trying to buck back against his face as he brings me back from my thoughts causing me cum again, but he moves away slapping me twice with the flogger on my ass a few of them hitting my pussy. He walks around to the front of me squatting to come face to face with me.

"Now I'm about to feed you baby. I want you to keep breathing through your nose for me and relax I am in control; can you do that for me?"

"Yeee... yes Ghost." I stutter coming to the realization of what he's about to do to me and if it's possible I become even wetter.

"That's my good slut." He groans. Dean connects out mouths in a heated sloppy kiss then stands and walks over to one of the cabinets pulling open a drawer, grabbing a bottle, that he pops the top on and squirts something all over his dick, and walks back over to me with his third leg pointing right at me like a diving rod guiding him home. Before he reaches me I hear a symphony of screams, moans, and fucks coming from Monty, Meira, and Jax. When I turn my head to look they still have her in the swing but now Monty is balls deep in her pussy while Jax is hitting it from the back.

"Well, they have clearly made up. Now let's get into our makeup session." He gives me a quick kiss then stands and without any further word shoves his large dick into my awaiting mouth right to the back of my throat initiating my gag reflex.

"Relax baby and remember your breaths, hmm fuck there you go." He starts with slow strokes against my tongue, my teeth occasionally grazing the thick under vein, and then he speeds up but I notice my throat is a lot more relaxed as he hits the thing in the back of my throat. I figure the oil he rubbed over his dick was a numbing oil so I get nasty with it and start to swallow around his dick taking him deeper.

"Gah dammit woman, fuck." He growls continuing his pursuit for ecstasy by way of my gawk gawk 3000 honey. He grabs a hand full of my freshly washed curls fucking my throat so deep and fast his balls start to smack at my chin until I swallow around his dick again and then they draw up tight.

"Fuck baby take your nut." He moans as I create suction and suck until he's shooting his warm, creamy, nut down my throat then his knees buckle as I keep going.

"Fuuuccckk." He growls in his deep gravely voice. He pulls out even though he is still hard as a brick. He begins unstrapping me from the bench then picks me up walking over to the large bed laying on his back and guiding me down his dick to rid him like he loves me to do. Monty is now laying next to us on the bed on his back but the bed is so damn big I cant even lean over and touch much of him. La'Meira hops on the bed going straight to taking his dick to the back of her throat while Jax whips himself off then gets behind her fat ass that's tooted up in the air. Jax begins eating her pussy from the back causing her to moan around Monty's dick and I swear it's the sexiest shit I've ever seen. I flatten my feet on the bed placing my hands on Dean's chest for leverage and start bouncing up and down tightening my walls as I rise. Dean grabs my hips helping me bounce harder and I cum for the third or fourth time this morning. At this point he has shattered my entire existence, and I don't know if I'm coming or going. This man has owned me everyday of our relationship even when I was fighting us being together.

"Mhmm shiiit Deeaann."

"Fuucckk right there Jax." Meira moans next to me as he has switched to fucking her pussy deep and fast, tearing her shit up. I keep bouncing going down on my knees to then leaning forward and twerking my ass on his dick. I lean back rocking my hips forward while using my hand to jack his dick on side of me simultaneously and that does it for him.

"Oh shit... shit Sweetness that's ch.. cheating fuckkk." He growls and I feel his nut painting my walls and I cum right with him. He pulls me forward with his dick still inside me giving me a passionate, tongue swirling kiss that causes my walls to clench around him. I hear a few fucks and grunts next to us then notice them laid out trying to catch their breath as well.

"Now that was a great start to us all making up." Dean announces lifting me up off the bed walking to the master bathroom.

Chapter Three

Dean Fredericks

After that session we take the girls into their master bathroom which is probably the size of some people's one bedroom apartment. I place Kelia on one toilet while Monty places Meira on the other, and yes these fools have two toilets in their bathroom. While the ladies relieve themselves I brush my teeth, Jax gets the shower going which I now notice has two rain shower heads above, another two handled on either side, with a bench the length of the back wall. The whole shower looks like it could fit at least six people maybe more. Jax takes my place at the sink brushing his teeth while Monty is at the other side and the ladies have already done the same. I walk in as Meira goes to sit on one side then Kelia and the fellas follow behind going on the opposite side. As I'm grabbing Meira's hand to stand under the shower head with me I hear Jax and Monty getting on Kelia.

"Ke you know how important you are to the family and you could've fixed all this months ago." Monty chastises her while holding her chin to look up at him I notice as I look over my shoulder. Jax is sitting on the bench and commands her to sit on his lap. I see the moment she looks at me for approval and I just simply nod, she's still getting use to this dynamic. I turn my attention back to my Lil Dove lifting her head up by the chin so I can look into her eyes when I say what I need too.

"Lil Dove don't ever and I mean ever go that long not speaking to me again. I love you woman and that was a hard three months with you and Kelia throwing everything off not communicating with us." I demand as I squat to lift her up, pressing her back to the shower glass, and she instinctively wraps her arms around my neck then legs around my waist. I thought we were close before but ever since we started this dynamic between the five of us I feel her engraved on my heart.

"I'm sorry Dean I guess I really did get stuck in that feeling of being mad and just didn't want to hear anyone out. You know I love you too Dean. I promise to communicate and ask for help next time." She apologies pecking my lips with a quick kiss. I swear I don't know if it's the steamed-up shower or the moans from my woman behind me, or the way Meira is looking at me now.

"I don't know if I should accept that apology, you really hurt my feelings." I fake pout then she reaches between us in the small gap only her small hand can fit through to grab at my dick that she can barely wrap her hand around and lines it up with her entrance.

"I'm not joking with you can never do that shit again. I can't function right without you. I need you and Kelia both Lil Dove." I reiterate holding her by the neck while slow entering her.

"Deeeaaann" She says breathlessly once I'm fully seated in her warm, wet, and tight pussy. I feel her pussy clench around me while I pull out then snap my hips forward in a quick harder thrust in an attempt to rearrange her thought process because she seriously has me fucked up. She licks my lips then I suck her tongue into my mouth and we start a slow sensual kiss that has me pumping into her harder.

"Remember your power, your place with us, and your beauty. You and that one over there better never forget it because next time we won't be so understanding or patient, understand?" Jax speaks life into her as she's bouncing on his dick and Monty has freed her mouth from his dick to answer.

"Ye... yes Smooth I understand." She moans calling him by his pet name. The ladies say he can talk the panties off a nun and I agree my brother has game.

"I'm with him Suga. Don't let us have a repeat of this mess you can open your mouth for this dick you can open it to express how you feel to all of us. You two mean the world to us, act like y'all know." Monty chastises her further while also speaking to Meira as he has his hand around Kelia's neck inciting a loud moan and her body to shiver. My Sweetness is close to cumming undone.

"You heard what he said right Lil Dove?" I question her putting my attention back on her and never losing my rhythm.

"Ye...yes Love Bug." She moans into my lips as I lean my forehead against hers. I feel her walls pulse around my dick confirming for me my Lil Dove is cumming undone for as me well. I deepen my strokes and rotate my hips initiating a rainfall of her juices down my dick and thighs. I'm not far behind her with the way she is gripping my dick.

"Fuck." I grunt out my release. I usually don't cum in her, but this session was too intense I couldn't pull out if I wanted to. I have my soulmate and my bestfriend back in full effect, it feels like my world has been set right on it's axis. We share one last kiss then we all get washed up, thankfully I'm not that much smaller than my brothers and Kelia is not that much smaller than Meira because a nigga was way to drained to walk back to the house. We all crash into the bed and wake up a few hours later to somebody's phone ringing then we realize all our phones are ringing. Everyone jumps up to figure out what's going on since we took our watches off.

"Hello." Jax answers the phone first and puts it on the speaker.

"Mr. Fredericks this is Principal Warren we have a situation at the school with Za'Meir and Darius. We need you all to come in right away." We were already grabbing wallets and keys to head out the door with the ladies right behind us. We all hop in one of our blacked-out Tahoe's and we all start to get text from the kids about what's going on.

"Fucking CPS trying to take my child. WHAT THE FUCK IS GOING ON?" Meira screams after reading a text from Mariah. We explain to her what happened this morning but didn't mention it because we thought it was handled. I read an email from our lawyer and just about crash the fuck out the moment we get out the truck.

"Brinx just emailed us this shit was handled so they shouldn't even be here messing with him. Brinx is on the way and contacting the bitch's supervisor now." Jax and I hold the door open for Meira and Kelia to walk through with Monty and the moment they both see the boys cuffed on the floor all hell just about breaks loose.

"Take those damn cuffs off our boys." Monty demands in a voice so calm but laced with pure venom at the school cops and then I notice the bitch from this morning with her little assistant holding a rag to his nose. The officers pick them both up and start to take the handcuffs off of them. The ladies instantly wrap the boys in their arms.

"Now why the hell are you even here?" I question the CPS agent.

"And why the hell were our boys handcuffed?" Jax stands next to me his face clear of emotion, but I feel the anger rolling off him.

"Let's go in my office." Principal Warren ushers us into his office just as the bell is sounding for the kids to switch to their second to last class of the day. We make sure our ladies sit and the three of us stand right behind them while the boys stand in the corner to our right. The CPS agent stands near the door with her assistant.

"Somebody better start answering our questions before I get active." Meira states in a calm even tone looking between the principal and the dumb bitch by the door. I am definitely going to allow my babies to play target practice with her ass after a few days of watching her.

"Ms. Fields came in with paperwork stating she had the right to remove Za'Meir from your custody and at that time he was already coming down the hall with Darius. When the gentleman with Ms. Fields reached for him after explaining to him why she was here Darius knocked him to the ground and then the officers here got involved."

"I want to see this so-called paperwork because I received an email from her supervisor and our family lawyer that this was settled." I explained while requesting said paperwork.

"There is no neglect happening in our home for any of our children. Yo mayonnaise sandwich bread ass only bothering us because we are a thriving black family, but your best bet is to find something safe to do cause messing with my family is not one of them." La'Meira comes out to play a bit but Jax and Monty rub her shoulder and the other grabs the back of her neck squeezing to calm her beast that's about to come out to play. I almost want to see it come out, I'd rather homeschool the kids anyway.

"Mrs. Fredericks it's no need for threats she is just doing her job." Principal Warren tries getting on Meira and that wasn't smart at all.

"Mr. Warren watch who you're talking to. My wife is not one of your students to chastise and if you were half as smart as you portray yourself to be you would know this is phony paperwork and not even signed by a real judge. We uncovered that in the five minutes we have been standing here." He reveals the information we have discovered after taking a photo of the paperwork and running it through a program Meira and Monty designed, those two together are fatal for everyone outside of our family.

Chapter Four

Kelia Fredericks

We sat in that office for over thirty minutes with this woman thinking she was taking our boy away. Brinx the family lawyer showed up with her supervisor after thirty minutes and all he did was tell her she was suspended pending investigation which pissed me off but looking at my family they clearly had something else planned. Whether they knew it or not I was riding with them this time. I am sick of being the timid and soft spoken Kelia, just letting people get away with everything, like my damn parents. When we get home, since we decided to check all the kids out early the drama continues for me as my parents are back blowing up my phone. They have been pissed with me since I left KC with Dean and our family to be there for Meira even though they are supposed to be so called Christians. I think I really pissed them off when I didn't tell them about Delia being born but they didn't want to accept my union with Dean so that was their faults. They have always been the judgmental types and I never understood that from the bible they made me read from front to back growing up.

"Yes mother." I answer the phone while moving around the kitchen to get some food ready for my family. Monty, Jax, and Meira are here, and the kids went over to the main house. Meira texted for the chef to make them lunch.

"Is that how you speak to your mother?"

"Ma I'm busy and I don't feel like arguing with you." I whisper into the phone, so everyone doesn't hear me. Dean has questioned why he hasn't met them yet, but I keep making excuses because I am so embarrassed of the people my parents are.

"Look your father and I want to meet our granddaughter, so you either show up here in the next week or we will be coming there. We are your family too." She gives me a ultimatum.

"We will be there Friday evening." Dean walks up behind me answering for me and I turn around shocked because I never even heard him move into the kitchen.

"Ok young man I will see you all Friday evening." She ends the call and now I'm face to face with my husband. We decided we didn't want to wait until Delia was born to get married so we had our wedding over by the barn before the horses were put in there. It was definitely my country dream wedding with beautiful flower arch ways made by Mama Fredericks, Mama Jennings even made my bouquet like she did Meira except mines was turquoise, white, burnt orange, and tan. I turn look up into my man's eyes and I see we about to have a serious conversation.

"I'm waiting." Is all he says to me and that's all he has to say.

"Just call everyone in. I guess I've been holding this in long enough." He calls for everyone to come in and they all sit at the island.

"Sweetness has something to tell us." He announces.

"It's about time, go ahead and spill babe." Meira states after hopping in the seat at the island Monty pulls out for her and Jax holds her hand to hop up.

"Why do you have to be so damn perspective bae, sheesh. So my parents are those so devoted Christians that turns their nose up at everybody around them like being Christians makes them better in someway so, they were adamant about me not moving here with Dean when everything happened with Meira. They were so against it when they found out I was not coming back they disowned me saying I was sinning by shacking up with Dean and that's why they weren't at the wedding. Then I found out by my aunt that they hired a private investigator to find out about all of you. That made them really lose their shit when the club was discovered and that I was pregnant by you. Now they are demanding to see Delia and I don't know how I really feel about that but since Dean has already agreed I guess we're going to see them."

"Well babe how about we make it a family thing but we leave the kids behind for the first meet up and if they seem good then we let them meet Delia." Meira suggest as she reaches across the island to rub my hand to comfort me.

"Meira's right. Let's meet up with them and if they acting stupid about us being a family they will not be in the presence of our child." Dean agrees with Meira and I just nod my head in agreement as well.

"Words woman." Dean turns my head towards him by my chin to answer properly.

"Yes that sounds like a plan." I verbalize.

"We have your back Suga, so the moment they start acting funny we out." Jax reassures me next and I never felt so supported until entering this family. We sit together laughing and talking until we all decide to have dinner at the main house. At dinner we fill the rest of the family in on the trip and it turns into an entire family trip to KC. Chase, Meech, and Marsh were upset about what my parents had done and declared to have my back as well, it was just so sweet. We had a time after dinner though, the men had us up and over their shoulder once the kids went upstairs heading to our Sinful Sanctuary. Our men turned us ever which way but loose. It's been a long week the men found out who the anonymous reporter was and this fool is about to catch hell before we leave. It's three am and the fellas are outside waiting on a delivery while Meira and I setup for it inside the large shed we have on the far west side of the compound, close to where the tree line starts. While setting up the last thing Meech requested for us to lay out we hear trucks pulling up. The wide shed doors start sliding open and in pull the guys with our special delivery. Dean as well as Monty walk in behind the trucks and close the sliding doors then walk over to us as the guys hop out the truck. Jax throws a pretty large man with a black bag over his head and hands cuffed behind his back out the trunk of the truck.

"Put that bitch in the chair on the plastic." Meira directs the men and they move at her command without a second thought. They proceed to cuff his legs then wrist to the chair.

"Sweetness you really don't have to be here for this, we have it handled." Dean comes up behind me rubbing his hands up and down my arms in a soothing motion and I lean my head back on his chest.

"He's right babe. You don't need to be tainted by this side of our family, Bree is here." Meira comes up wrapping our hands together and giving me a quick peck on the lips.

"I'm over everyone always handling the hard things for me, it's time I pull my weight in this family and not just the easy stuff." I declare giving them each a kiss then walk off to the dumb ass that thought it was a good idea to try and separate our family then snatch the bag off his head.

"Well hello Mr. James." I greet the boys football coach who is blinking his eyes fast trying to adjust to the light in here.

"So Drew you thought it was a smart idea to make up lies about my family and attempt to take my son away from me." She spits pure venom then reaches back then collides her fist with his jaw and we hear the crack of bones.

"Fuck that was hot." Money groans from the left of the room and I hear Monty as well as Jax agree with him.

"Meechy baby you said you had something special for me to use?" She asks as I come to stand next to her and Meech walks over to the table grabbing a syringe then hands it to Meira.

"That will completely paralyze his movements, but he will feel absolutely everything you decide to do to him and it last about an hour or two then his organs start to shut down one by one. So, he will either die from the pain you inflict on him or slowly suffocate to death once his lungs stop working." He explains leaning down to kiss her on the cheek then walks back to where the guys are all standing. They are forming a half circle behind us, all looking murderous and ready to jump if they think we feel the least bit in danger.

"Well babe do you want to do the honors?" She inquires looking at me as I stand to her right holding the needle out to me.

"My pleasure." I respond taking the need then removing the cap and walk over to him stabbing him in the leg. I push the silver liquid into him and his body starts to twitch then he throws his head back.

"Oh yea I forgot to mention it will burn as it moves through the body." Meech adds in with a chuckle behind us. I step back putting the syringe on the table then look at the different blades, pliers, and other torture devices Meira laid out.

"Well you can't talk or scream which is absolutely lovely because I really don't want to hear all that damn noise and lets be real its not much that you can say to justify your fuck up." Meira taunts grabbing a knife on the table and gliding it against his eye lid cutting so deep its hanging on by a small piece. I thought I'd be more grossed out but honestly, I'm more intrigued than anything at how it's still holding on. I feel the urge to cut him so I grab a scalpel off the table and slash his arm with it then his face, stepping back to look at my handy work.

"Oh, I am fuckin the shit out of her tonight." Dean groans behind me and I turn to see him biting on his bottom lip sending heat straight to my core. I turn to get back to the job at hand.

"I'm still trying to wrap my mind around your thought process though. Like you really thought you were going to have yo lil jump off take my son, bring him to you and you were going to have him put in the foster systems somewhere if I didn't agree to be with you?" Meira lays out the information we were able to obtain from Ms. Fields yesterday in such a cold and detached tone it sends chills down my spine. He just moves his eyes as he's paralyzed from the neck down.

"Yea your lil fuck buddy gave us the whole play, which she apparently was going to double cross you on and hit us up for some money instead" I fill in the rest of our rendezvous. Meech created a serum that would make her susceptible to telling the truth then gave her one that mimicked amnesia but was permanent for all her short-term memories.

"She was never going to be yours, she's ours always will be." I declare while plunging a large butcher knife into his shoulder then grab the rim of Meira's sweatpants she is wearing to turn her towards me then by the collar of her shirt to bring her closer. I cup the back of her head as I connect our lips with my other hand sliding into her pants then rubbing her clit with two of my fingers. She moans into my mouth, and I hear the guys grunting in the back. I break our kiss leaning our foreheads together as I slide my fingers through her slick lips.

"Ke. Mmhmm." She moans as I push my fingers into her honeypot then push them against her G spot repeatedly until she cums all over my hand.

"Ok enough of this shit." Monty announces and the fellas agree. He grabs the torch off the table and Dean picks up a poker stick placing it into the flames of the torch. It's getting so hot the metal starts to turn reddish orange and before anyone can do or say anything else Monty hands it over to Jax who then pushes it straight through the coach's heart.

"Hey Money, Tru y'all got this?" Monty questions throwing Meira over his shoulder, before I can even brace myself Dean has me over his walking towards the shed doors.

"We gotcha big bro." They dapped and headed to handle what remained as we went to have our insides rearranged by our men.

Chapter Five

Dean Fredericks

We are all hoping on the plane this morning dragging like a motherfucker after our late or early morning session in our Sinful Sanctuary. The girls all walked on the plane with those sexy fuckin sundresses, asses just giggling, tittes sitting pretty with their shades on, each one with different braided styles since it's well into the spring which is still hot around these parts. My brothers are all dressed in some version of basketball shorts and white tees, which the brother group has grew into eight from six with Money and Tru. They are both almost done building their homes but have been staying in the main house as everyone has at some point. The flight back to KC was quick and silent with everyone asleep, the moment we land we all hop in our waiting trucks with all of us heading to Monty's crib since it's the biggest. Our parents will be flying in later on today with all the kids since the earliest we wanted to take them out of school was one o'clock so they don't miss much. We get in and of course Monty had his chef here to whip up breakfast.

"Damn I didn't realize I was so hungry." Jax states leaning back in his chair rubbing his belly and I can't do anything but laugh cause this big ass nigga always hungry.

"Ok I need a nap. We are to meet with my parents at The Fredericks around six- thirty but before that mama

Fredericks and dem will be here in around three ." Kelia informs us all as she stretches her arms wide and yawning sitting to my right next to Jax.

"Say less Sweetness." I agree standing from my seat going to pull her out. I know it's been a long week and it's not even over yet.

"I mean actually sleep babe. My pussy hasn't recovered from the past three days." She giggles hitting my arm and I laugh too. Since finally getting our women back we have been on their asses like a bee to honey every chance we get.

"Fine sleep only." I chuckle. I lean over Meira's shoulder giving her a kiss on the cheek as we make our way to one of the rooms. I hear everyone else say they need some sleep as well before we pick one of the eight bedrooms this fool had but now makes sense. Hell it was only eight in here he had another four in the guest house out back. Kelia and I take a quick shower then slide up under silk burgundy sheets on the king size bed.

"Talk to me Sweetness, I feel the tension rolling off you. I have for awhile but wanted to give you the space to come to me first. No more hiding." I address the cloud that's been hanging over us for the past year now.

"Babe I just never thought we'd become such a fast couple and bond so well then have my parents be so against it. Let's not mention the unorthodox relationships we are all in and I occasionally have moments of doubt or insecurity with everything. There that's all of it." She releases her feelings on to me as she lays comfortably on my chest rubbing her fingers in a circle.

"I need you to hear me and hear me good. I love Meira she's apart of my heart always will be but you ma'am are embedded in every fiber of my fucking being. Not having you is like trying to breathe with one working lung. Baby I'd follow your soul to hell and bring it back if I had to. So please don't ever underestimate my love for you." She turns her head up towards me pouting her lips for a kiss I happily give.

"I know babe but thank you for the reminder."

"I'll remind you every day of our lives if I have to and not just with words."

"I would like to hear about how you and Meira did meet and become friends though." I knew eventually she'd want full detail and it's cool I been ready to tell her.

"The event was getting boring, all the tech was either not well tested, or not useful for my PI firm or Monty's security firm. I was just about to tell my case manager that came with me we were leaving until this glowing, chocolate goddess caught my eye as she stood talking with one of the unimportant salesmen at a booth. She was wearing these dark green linen, pleated, loose fitting pants with a off white silk long sleeve blouse unbuttoned just enough to give a peak at her large breast. I mean she was thick in all the right places with her short ass. She had simple gold statement pieces around her neck and wrist. She had the look on her beautiful face that said she was done talking to the fool in her face but was trying not to be rude, so I took that as my queue to save her." I looked down at her to make sure this wasn't bothering her but she was smiling and rubbing up and down my abs so I continued.

"I got her away from the salesmen which she thanked me for but I didn't want her to leave so I asked her to grab a drink with me in the back and we ended up talking and flirting for hours. We ended up exchanging numbers pretty much talking everyday whether it was through text or video calls. We linked up a few times just having dinner or visiting this game room near her when she stayed in Florida. It was about a year or more later I had just left dinner with my brothers when she called me with the most guttural heart wrenching scream that made me whip my car to the nearest parking lot to try and get her to calm down." I had to pause because just remembering that scream was doing something to my spirit. Kelia noticed hugged me tighter then rubbed her face over my heart and I kissed the top of her head.

"I was already getting to a bad head space since it was close to the anniversary of my dad's death so my mind went to worst case scenario. I thought someone had hurt her or the kids. While I was trying to get her to calm down enough I was getting our pilot together so I can get to her and telling my brothers I had something to handle but wouldn't be back for a few days. I hate to say but when she told me it was her best friend that something had happened to I was kinda relieved."

"You were just glad it wasn't her, I get that." Kelia says and I knew she would understand my thoughts process.

"Exactly by the time she told me everything I was already boarding the jet heading to her. I stayed with her and the kids for about two weeks. I hadn't experienced that level of peace in a long, long time. She slept in the bed with me most night balled up in my side sometimes crying softly till she fell asleep or some nights we talked until she could. One of the nights I told her about how I was the one that found my father with the needle sticking out of his arm, eyes rolled in the back of his head, drool coming from the side of his mouth, stiff, cool to the touch and just slumped to the side. He had recently moved onto something stronger when the pills stopped working to give him the high, he was trying to attain. I told her how that shit was seared into my brain and how I wished at that time I was as detached emotionally as my brother Monty. Mom had just started teaching him emotional queues around that time because a boy in his class had died on the playground and he just stood there. He didn't cause it but he didn't scream in fear, cry, nothing just looked at him with curiosity in his eyes."

"That was terrible baby, damn I can't imagine how that has scared you." She rolls on top of me hugging me tighter than before.

"I was scared for a while that I would end up like him but those two weeks I spent with her, we both were trying to find ways to laugh more than cry, keep the kids upbeat after losing their God mother, and just holding each other healed so many parts of me I didn't know that could or needed to be. Everyday after those two weeks were even more healing. At that time she was the only person who saw me and I threw my sexual desires for her away. She spoke life into me and guarded me from shit I couldn't see with her intuition hell her love for me. You could say she healed me so I could be with you like I am now. So yes, we have something deeper than a normal best friend relationship but just remember it's not what we have Sweetness." Just rehashing all this makes me feel closer to my wife but now I need one of my bestfriends hugs too.

"Go get your hug baby. That was a lot you shared with me and I'm glad you did. I understand you and her even more. I appreciate knowing if anything ever happens to me someone I trust and is capable will be able to take care of you. Now shoo get your hug I'm getting my nap." She expresses after kissing me on the chest then rolling over to get comfortable. I whisper in her ear I love her then kiss her on the shoulder and head out to find my bestie which isn't hard since she's downstairs with all of our kids and Monty and Jax playing with them all.

"Hi daddies princess." I greet Delia who's on her back on the play mat looking at the sun and stars hanging for her to grab. I pick her up and sit next to Meira and just like always she knows just what I need.

"What upset my Love Bug?" She questions as she wraps her arms around me as much as she can then kisses me on the cheek and lays her head on my shoulder.

"No one. Me and Kelia just had the conversation about how we got so close." She knows what that brung up for me so she hugs me again this time not letting go for a few minutes.

"I remember when she finally told us, I wanted to punch you Lil brother." Jax states sitting across from us on the floor bouncing Junior on his leg.

"I did too. You could've talked to us about how you were feeling. I know I don't always comprehend emotions well but you're my Lil brother man and you were hurting all that time." Monty says burping Jackson while Ayomi plays on the other baby mat.

"Bro it wasn't you, either of you. Hell I didn't even realize how much I needed to get it out or that I was holding that much in until I was holding this one and it all just rushed to the surface like a damn tsunami. You know the effect Meira has, she just silently pulls things outta ya." I kiss the top of her head.

"You're not wrong she's helped me acknowledge some of my own emotions towards our father hell myself for always being father figure since he did what he did. Hell I didn't even realize I had any ill feelings towards it but after having one of our chill nights on the back patio at the old house." She signals for Monty to come next to her after giving me another kiss on the cheek. He comes and lays his head on her lap and she runs her hands through his dreads while Jackson lays on his chest.

"You really do have a way with the mess Phoenix. Hell she got me the same way but it brung out stuff about the army I was suppressing. Damn woman had me in tears by the time I finished letting everything out. Hell come to think about it I don't even think she really even said much just held me and kissed my cheek." Jax recounts how Meira got him to release his emotions. She really is the center of this family.

Chapter Six

Kelia Fredericks

All my babies fell asleep lying on the floor with the kids, I had to wake them and call the big kids in to grab the babies so we all could get dressed. Dean and I just finished getting ready and we are going downstairs to meet with the family.

"Aight now, looks like Suga showing out tonight." Monty compliments me as we make it to the bottom of the stairs and everyone else agrees. I have on a burnt orange bandage sleeveless jumpsuit that cuts a little low in the breast area and is hugging all my curves just enough. I decided on my rose gold heart locket collar, matching bracelet, and ring set Dean bought me recently. Each piece has Dean's name engraved on the inside along with the date we met. I put on one of my wigs Bree made me that is jet black, with a side part, and big bouncy curls that goes past my shoulders on. Complete with natural makeup, nude lip, my black clutch and black wedges, I must admit I'm looking good.

"I know all of you aren't talking. I have one fine ass family." I returned the compliment going from the men to the women licking my lips. It's insane how all our perfumes and colognes compliments each other but made for such a fuck me scent. Dean is looking exceptionally fuckable with the silk long sleeve button up the same color as my jumpsuit that is still a bit tight around his arms even though he got it in larger size, then the black slacks that are just his size displaying just a hint of that third leg I love so much with the black suede loafers, a nice simple gold watch that clearly cost more than my whole wardrobe, and a couple gold chains completed his look. That beard was glistening after I moisturized it and he had a fresh cut so you know those waves were so shiny and deep you might get seasickness.

"Before we go, I want y'all to know how much I really appreciate all of you coming with us on this trip and to this dinner. I also don't want any of you to act any differently then you normally would. That really goes for you three, I know the world doesn't really accept the type of relationship you have and it's bad enough you're black as well as successful. Basically just be yourselves if my parents don't approve fuck em, ok." I inform them all but making sure that Monty, Meira, and Jax understand most of all.

"I hear you babe but you two tone down the serial killer vibes before I lock y'all asses up somewhere." Meira pins Marsh and Bree with that mom side eye that lets you know you done fucked up royally. They give her a tight nod then put their heads down because they know they've been caught and called out in front of everyone. We all hop into our awaiting vehicles, the fellas thought it was best to have our drivers on duty tonight just in case we may need to get turned up a bit after meeting with my family. They even sent a car service for my parents as well as my brother and sister that are coming with their wife and husband, which I'm sure their boogie asses loved. We arrived pulling up in the back of the restaurant then taking the private entrance through their office.

"Good evening bosses your guest are already seated in the private dining room and have been served drinks only. Would you like to put your drinks in as well?" Our private host greets the guys and we all provide our drinks then we are escorted to our private room. Entering the room and spotting my parents immediately with their typical nice nasty facial expressions makes me want to turn around and say fuck this but I feel Dean squeeze my hand.

"Well our daughter has finally arrived." My father is the first to speak.

"Hi dad and mother." I greet them dryly first giving them a church hug as my father still has that smile on his face that doesn't quite reach his eyes. It means two things he trying to be nice but he is secretly judging everyone in the room and so Is mother. I side hug my siblings as we have never been close with me being the youngest by four years.

"Well, everyone this is Dean Fredericks, my husband." I introduced him first as everyone decided to stay out in the hall to give us just a moment to ourselves.

"Nice to meet you Mr. & Mrs. Black. You as well Percy and Shannon." Dean greets holding his hand out to shake my father's which he hesitates to reach out at first which is strike one for me. I am sure his ego is chipped a bit at the size of Dean compared to his slim five ten frame and the firm handshake he gives him chipped it even further. My father is a firm believer that you can tell a lot about a man by his handshake, and I know he just realized Dean is not to be fucked with in any sense of the word. He shakes my mother hand next then goes down the line. By the time he finishes introducing himself everyone else walks and standing on either side of us.

"These are my brother Montavius with his wife and my best friend La'Meira and Jax, that's Chase and his fiancé Kenya, Demetrius, Tru, Blake, and the youngest of the bunch Marshall and his fiancé Briana." He goes down his long list of siblings and I see the pride in Tru as well as Money when he simply introduces them as his siblings. The hostess comes in with help to deliver all of our drinks and I'm glad we didn't have to wait long because I can see the look on my parent's face changing from trying to keep the peace. I'm sure they caught on to how he introduced our family throuple. We take our seats Dean pulling mines out and the dead ringer for the three of them is Monty as well as Jax pulling out Meira's chair then sitting on either side of her. I see the moment my sister catches on with her messy ass but head off the stupid shit that was about to come out her mouth quick.

"So, mom how has the church fundraisers been going?"

"They are doing pretty good. They would be doing a lot better if you were still in charge of them" I was ok with her throwing that shot as long as she didn't speak on anything else. I would like us to at least make it through dinner before all hell breaks loose. The server soon comes in taking everyone's order and that is when the first level of bull shit starts.

"So, you men are proud of what you do for a living?" My mother starts in first.

"Ma don't –"

"No Sweetness it's ok. We are very proud of what we do. My older brothers and I retired from Marines first then we all collectively own one of the top security and PI firms. Yes, we also own two different types of adult clubs, but we also own the car service you rode to our restaurant in, along with a construction company, rental properties and much more. I'm sure the PI you had look into me found those as well and they all allow me to give my beautiful wife and kids the life we have. Again, yes we are very proud." He leans back in his chair placing his arm across the back of mines then rubs his thumb in a circular motion more to calm himself than me on my shoulder and it's only because she mentioned his brothers, he could care less about them attacking his character. Thankfully the server comes back with the appetizers first and everyone digs in, but I see my mother giving them the side eye.

"So why don't you have a woman, Jax is it?" I almost choked on my damn infused cheese sticks cause of this bitch, but I have a trick for her ass.

"Hey, Brandon, how was your trip to LA last month, eventful was it?" I question her husband who apparently has been cheating on her for the past few months. If she was a better sister, I would've gladly given her the information I had Dean look up on all of them before we got here for just this situation.

"Brandon, what trip is she talking about? You told me you were on a business trip in Chicago last month" She was about to get real hyped on him but he whispers something in her ear that makes her shut her trap quick. Meira and I share a quick giggle as the servers come in to clear the appetizer plates and the other comes in with our dinner. It has already been a tense thirty minutes so I'm hoping they keep their traps shut while we enjoy this dinner. I'm glad but partially not that we all chose to due the infused side of the menu cause Meira has started reaching over Jax's lap and rubbing my leg under the table. Dean thinks the shit is funny and had the audacity to connect their hands together for a moment in my lap. We make it through dinner and some of us are eating dessert and that's when I know it's no more avoiding the shit hitting the fan.

"Here babe have some of mines." Meira walks over to offer Jax some of her double chocolate cake as he stands at the bar chatting with Monty and Money. He happily eats the piece off the fork then grabs her by the waist to pull her in between him and Monty. She feeds Monty some of the cake next and then she eats some as well and now they both have one hand on her but I can tell they are trying to control themselves since I see the look of lust in their eyes. I am sitting next to my mother facing them talking about the upcoming charity ball my black ass will not be attending but I am letting her think I will.

"What type of mess is this?" My father questions standing from his seat next to my mother and I hear my sister giggling like a stupid little schoolgirl.

"What are you talking about dad?" I play like I didn't see what he just saw because the weed has kicked in and I am liable to say something crazy.

"You know damn well what I'm talking about. Are those three to... together?" His face is turned up into the craziest frown showing just how disgusted he is by what he just witnessed.

"No Monty is married to Meira and her and Jax are in a committed relationship. Before you say something crazy of course they don't touch each other they are brothers." I feel like I'm defending my family for their choices, and I am not feeling it one bit. These muthafucka's better not ruin my damn high or I am going to flip on them.

"What type of sinful mess are you raising my poor granddaughter around and don't think I didn't catch them two playing handsy in your lap earlier. Is this slut sleeping with your husband too?" My mother calls out the antics that have been going been on all night but her calling Meira a slut almost makes me slap the taste out her mouth. I never understood how she could judge others when my brother isn't even my fathers and mind you they have been together since high school.

"Watch your mouth mother." I stand up from my seat next to her then walk over to Meira then we lock hands, and she tells me it's ok but I'm not trying to hear that shit.

"Oh no dad I think she's sleeping with her. I told you she never gave up her sinning ways." My bitch ass sister always hated how our parents doted on me growing up like I asked for the shit. I still remember the day she thought she finally found something that would make them put her mediocre ass on a pedestal. I was at my sweet sixteen party and this chick I was crushing on came. I was too geeked that she actually showed but that was dampened out the moment my sister caught us kissing in the bathroom. It was so unexpected she had given me this beautiful necklace with my initials, apparently, she had been crushing on me too but thought I was only into boys. I was just so excited that I gave her a quick kiss but it turned into more real fast and just as I was really enjoying it here comes my shiatzu faced ass sister. She ran from the door like someone said it was time for second desserts wit her fat ass, straight to my parents who were talking to members of the congregation shouting about me kissing a girl. My parent lost their shits when they saw me and her coming out the bathroom with my lip gloss on her lips and my face flush from our kiss but now from embarrassment as well.

"Yes, I have a special connection with Meira. She makes me feel good to be my real self and so does my husband. Hell, our whole family does. They accept me for who I am not judge me." I reveal what is going on between us all and just how loved I am in my new family.

"No, I will not allow you heathens to send my daughter and granddaughters soul to hell. I told you we took her out too soon Charles" She shouts, getting angry and I can't help but tense up at the mention of the damn place they sent me after my birthday party. I didn't even have time to tell my friends goodbye before they shipped me off.

"Wait where the hell did you send her and it better not be where I think?" Meira is getting pissed. I can feel the heat rolling off her and not the one that I love feeling from her.

"You might just be right another six months might've set her right and she wouldn't be walking down this path of sin." My father upholds what my mother just shared. I have been running away from the memories of that place for years.

"Tell me now Kelia did your parents send you to one of those conversion camps and don't lie to me?" Meira gently grabs my chin turning my head towards her and the memories flashing in my mind start bringing tears to my eyes. She quickly wraps her arms around me as I start to break as my mind keeps replaying the beatings I had to endure or the constant isolation if I didn't answer a question the way they wanted.

"I told y'all back then she faked that whole suicide just so you would come get her." Before I could even think of anything to say or do Bree was going upside my sister's head while all I could do is sob into Meira's shoulder. It was like the pain wouldn't stop, it felt like an eighteen-car pileup and each car was a piece of me that broke the six months that I was there.

"Get off my daughter you floozy." I hear my mom shout at Bree who's still going ham on my sister and shouting all types of profanities. Marsh finally decides to grab her off her but the final blow she lands isn't a physical one it's about her cheating ass husband who's trying to help her ass up off the floor.

"Are seriously going to let her attack your sister like that?"

"Stop talking to my wife. As a matter of fact consider this dinner over and understand this you will never see her again and won't step a foot near our daughter. You can find your own way home." Dean declares turning to grab me from Meira and Jax who were both holding me up at this point then he lifts me bridal style walking towards the exit but stops the moment my parents shout the dumbest shit possible.

"You can keep her filthy behind, but we will not allow you to corrupt our granddaughter even if we have to file for custody of her. You aren't fit to be parents." That shit made Monty snap and in the blink of an eye he had my father's feet dangling from the floor with his massive hands wrapped around his throat cutting off his air supply. My brother attempts to go aid our father but is quickly stopped by Jax that has this evil grin on his face. Dean continues to walk out the door with Meira at our side, leaving the others behind and part of me hopes they kill all of their asses, but I know without my word they won't do it. Right now, I can't even form a sentence. My screams and heavy tears have slowed to sniffles, but I am completely out it at this point. I feel like I'm having an outer body experience.

Chapter Seven

Dean Fredericks

It's about eleven o' clock now and we have been home for a few hours. It took a while for Kelia to calm down enough to fall asleep. It took for me and Delia to cuddle up with her which I was perfectly fine with, I just wanted my baby to be ok. I slid out a few minutes ago after putting Delia down in the baby room with the triplets so I can sit with my brothers on the back patio and light us a joint to further calm my damn nerves because if I don't her whole family is going to the forest my wolves haven't eaten heavy in a while.

"Man bruh." Is all I can get out. Processing this shit is a lot harder then I thought it would be. I never imagined her parents were that fuckin cruel to her.

"I know man. Her parents are some seriously fucked up individuals to send their own daughter to a place like that." Monty states as he passes me the joint he's holding. I take a few puffs then lean back in my chair and scratch my head with my other hand.

"Really fucked up. We had some girls even boys at the sanctuary that were rescued from those type of camps. Hell sometimes they were more beaten and tortured then our trafficked victims were." Tru states. That didn't do anything to kill the volcano that is close to erupting inside of me.

"Don't trip D I'm already on it. If she doesn't give us the word on her parents I already have the system tracking down the camp she could've been placed at along with anyone that worked their during that time." Jax attempt at soothing my anger actually helps some. My baby will get retribution one way on another.

"Is it me or my wife's freaky powers were at work tonight." Monty jokes and we all laugh cause she really did strike again at pulling some shit out of one of us.

"Wait what's Meira's powers?" Money ask passing around another joint.

"Don't worry you will feel it soon enough. Just know when it does its OK to cry nigga we won't judge you one bit." I inform him laughing even harder at his confused and worried face. While sitting there shooting the shit I get a text from Meira saying she just prayed over Kelia using her sage to help balance her energy. All I can do is smile and send her the kissy face emoji.

"What you smiling about?" Chase questions as he's handing me the joint.

"Meira just texted me that she prayed over my wife. I swear that woman is heaven sent."

"That she is brother that she is." Before we can start up another conversation after sitting in silence for a bit we hear the sliding door open.

"Chocolate Bear, Big Daddy it's time for bed." Meira says seductively then turns around dropping her silk robe on the floor and sashaying back towards the stairs leading to their room. Them fools don't say bye or nothing. They just hop up from their seats and head into the house picking up her robe as they go.

"These three." Chase chuckles.

"Those three freaky shit is the last thing on my mind. The list of people against our family is growing and that shit is not sitting right with me." I confide in my brothers the shit that's started to plague my brain.

"Well we can take one thing off our family list-" Tru starts but Chase cuts him off by hitting him in the chest.

"Do that shit again nigga." Tru warns Chase while rubbing his chest.

"Speak before I get pissed off and toss all of you over the damn rail." I stand my voice getting low sounding even deeper than it already is.

"Look big bro we just wanted to take something off the family's plate. You, Monty, and Jax having newborns then Meira as well as Kelia weren't speaking to any of you like that which just made shit more stressful for y'all." Meech starts to explain.

"Facts and you guys were made for each other seeing y'all so disconnected fucked with us so we had to do something to help out." Money adds in. I feel pride that my brothers will do what's needed to keep our family in tact even in my absence.

"Look I'm glad y'all handled a problem for the family but which was it?"

"We got rid of Calder." Marsh finally speaks up.

"Ok that's a major piece off the board fellas. Damn. You sure he's gone though?"

"For sure. We put a few bullets in him then surrounded the house he was hold up in then set it on fire." Chase explains.

"Yea we stayed until it was burnt to a crisp and no one made it out." Tru finishes.

"That nigga should have never messed with our Queen." Money declares leaning back in his seat as he puffs on his joint. I had to pull them up one by one for a hug. Calder was a serious threat with his connections in government even if he was crooked, I'm sure he had enough wealthy clients to help him harm our family. I can breathe a bit and I'll let the arakunrin nla know along with bestie later. We sit shooting the shit for a few more minutes before we hear a scream pierced through the air so desperate and filled with fear all of our instincts are kicked into overdrive sending us running into the house to figure out where it came from. By the time we make it to the stairs Monty, Jax, and Meira are rushing to cover themselves while coming out of their room. Chase runs to check if it was Kenya while Marsh ran into Bree who is already coming out their room since we know it's not the babies or the big kids as they are in the guest house with our parents. The moment the thought registers I take off down the hall to my room, swinging the door open I find a screaming Kelia drenched in sweat tossing around in the bed, and I rush over to her.

"Wait be gentle with waking her she's stuck in a nightmare and a terrible one at that." Meira cautions me as she steps further in the room with the rest of our family but they stand back.

"Sweetness listen to my voice baby and wake up for me. Whatever is in that dream can't hurt you anymore." I coach her to wake and she finally does as I rub up then down on her arms as well as kiss her cheek. She jumps up and looks around in fear but then realizes where she is.

"What... what the hell happen?" She questions as she relaxes more into my touch.

"You were having a nightmare and clearly a bad one it took you a few minutes for you to come out of it. Do you want to tell us what happened?" I rub her cheek with my knuckles, and she turns to kiss my hand.

"I... I guess."

"You don't have to if you're not ready babe." Meira assures her as she gets in the bed on the other side then starts rubbing her exposed shoulder with her cheek.

"No... no I think I need to. I haven't had these nightmares in years so clearly meeting my parents and siblings triggered them since I never really dealt with them."

"Ok we will step out." Chase starts to leave as well as the others but she stops them.

"Wait can all of you stay. You guys are my family and it's no other people I would rather share this with." She expresses herself and everyone finds somewhere to sit or lay.

"So, the dream itself was me being locked up in the room they use to call the *dark room* on the conversion camp. It was about the size of porta potty made from brick, with only a small opening at the top for air, and light. They would leave us in there for days on end." She takes a breath, and I hear a few what the fucks coming from some of the fam which is the exact thing I was thinking. I give Monty and Jax the look and they both know it's full force when we get back home.

"I would take the dark room over their version of baptisms. They would bind our hands and feet then push us into the pool they had on site. They only let us up when we stopped fighting which of course meant we either stopped breathing or we learned to hold our breath long enough to be considered clean. It was also considered a cleansing of our demons."

"Aww fuck no I'm fucking their asses up. How the hell can you do that to a person let alone your child." Bree shouts jumping from her seat on Marsh's lap in the arm chair in the corner of the room but he pulls her back down to his lap and she apologizes for her outburst.

"Hell, I haven't even told the craziest part. My own sister is the reason I was sent to begin with. On my sixteenth birthday a girl I liked from school came and we end up making out in the bathroom. This bitch caught us and ran straight to our parents to snitch. I didn't even get to say bye to my friends, open gifts, pack a bag or nothing. Straight from my party on a six-hour drive to the camp, they shipped my damn clothes to me a few days later. I was stuck there for six months and it just got so bad I just wanted to end it all, so I tried to. They had these wraps that they would usually use on the boys that had these needle points and depending on how bad they were determined how tight they tied it around their arm or leg. I took one of them and wrapped it tight around my thigh after taking a bottle of one of the counselors sleeping pills and just left it there hoping to bleed out, but they eventually found me then called my parents to come get me." She finished explaining then leaning forward to lay her head on my chest and I just hold her as the tears fall. Meira and I make a silent declaration that we are offing her damn sister in the worse way possible. We all sit in silence for a few minutes just letting all that shit settle in us. After a while everyone starts to get up and say good night.

"Wait can you all sleep in here tonight? Is that ok babe?" She looks around at everyone that was coming to hug her and say good night.

"It's cool with me." I answer and they all leave the room but after a few minutes one by one they come back with their pillows and blankets. I get in the bed sandwiching her between me and Meira who was about to get out the bed to lay with my brothers but they made her stay in bed. Kelia was able to get a few hours of sleep before Delia woke up crying for her morning bottle and she wouldn't let me get up to feed her but she did come back to bed with her. We stayed in bed most of the day everyone staying in our room until our big babies woke up then we took it to the living room. I can tell the support of the family is what's keeping my Sweetness from breaking down and I appreciate them more than they know.

Chapter Eight

Kelia Fredericks

It's been about a month since I let everyone in on the worst six months of my life and I haven't felt this light in a long time. Things at home aren't back to normal, they are even better because I am better mentally. I do feel like everyone else is either walking on eggshells or hiding something from me and it ends tonight I decide the moment I walk into the main house for our family game and dinner night with Dean as well as the kids.

"Let me talk to y'all Mama Fredericks you too." She didn't sleep with us that night, but Dean and I had a talk with all of them the next morning. To say they didn't take everything well is putting it mildly.

"Yes babe." Meira speaks first coming over to me, wrapping me in a hug, then a quick peck on the lips as we normally greet each other at this point.

"So, who wants to speak up first as to why the hell everyone has been acting weird around me and don't even try to lie." I look at each of them and wait for someone to respond.

"Look Sweetness we didn't know how you would feel about the things we have been doing lately. I know you recently stepped into the darker side of some of the shit we do but it's never hit this close to home for you." Dean beats around the bush which is kind of annoying me now. Mama Fredericks notices and decides to step in.

"Look baby girl after you told all of us what happened to you on behalf of your parents' ignorance we set something in motion plus they actually tried filling paperwork to get custody of Delia, but we shut that shit down fast." That was a blow I wasn't expecting. I know my parents can be a pill but to actually try and take my child from me they have fucked up beyond repair. I was thinking about just letting them live in misery but they are seriously pushing my damn buttons.

"And why the hell did no one tell me about this?" I question everyone but look directly at Dean first.

"First, I wanted to see if it was anything to worry about and you have been so much lighter since that night. I didn't want to dull that at all unless it was absolutely necessary." He attempts to justify holding that from me but I will deal with his ass at home later. Sometimes he forgets he's taught me how to be submissive and how to be dominant, which is something I will always love about him most men's egos are to big for them to let a woman dominate them.

"So what is that you guys have been doing?" I question again for clarification since no one has flat out told me what's going on.

"We tracked down the camp you went to and it's still open. The so call counselors that were there during your time are gone and we have been tracking them down one by one." Monty finally tells me the whole truth.

"So have you found any of them?"

"Only two so far. My team has been tracking their every move. One stays in Georgia the other stays in Michigan." Tru gives me the other details.

"Well, there were six of them that I had contact with on a regular basis. I can't remember their names, but I'd never forget their faces. What about the camp?" I inform them as my face turns into a sinister grin once I decide what I want to do when they track them all down.

"I know that look we have many things you can do to them babygirl to claim back you power when you are ready." Mama Fredericks comforts me with her words and a hug filled with love and safety I never received from my own mother.

"We can take it down if you want, over twenty of my rescues have been safely relocated in their new homes, so I have room for some at Texas sanctuary." Tru offers and I nod for him to do so.

"There is a question of you parents and your sister though babe. We all want to off their asses but only if you approve." Meira looks over at me bracing herself for me to lash out at her for even mentioning possibly killing my parents, but I have no intention of doing so.

"I haven't decided about them yet. I know for sure they are cut off from my life permanently. The only family I need is you guys and no more tip toeing around me either. I'm not some fragile porcelain doll that is going to break, understood?" They all nod their responses, and we file out of Jax's and Monty's downstairs office then hop on the elevator to ride to the second-floor game room where the kids await. We have a night full of fun, just laughing with our kids, and eating great food. The chef put her foot, elbows, and knees in the dinner she prepared. It was funny seeing Monty negotiate with Meira on how many days she could come cook dinner for them back when she was hired, that woman does not play about her kitchen. They eventually came to a compromise of three days a week sometimes if none of us felt like cooking for our family nights. Something told me after that night I should have blocked all of their numbers, but I didn't think they would reach out but clearly no such luck because here they go calling.

"Why are you calling me Mrs. Black." I greet my so-called mother the moment the call connects.

"That is no way to greet your mother young lady." Her lame ass attempt at trying to scold me makes me chuckle.

"Like I said what do you want?" I reiterated.

"I want to schedule a date with my granddaughter. She's five months and you have yet to let me see her and that's just not right." She tries to guilt trip me and that shit goes through one ear and out the other.

"I told you before I left the restaurant and so did my husband. You will never have access to any of my children and I know about your lil failed attempt at filing for custody of her. Nice try but if that is all it's time for me to get my kids ready for school and don't ever call me again. Consider yourself dead to me." I end the call and went about fixing my family breakfast as I hear Dean coming in with our little princess.

"Good morning my Sweetness." He greets me when he gets close enough he kisses me on my shoulder while bouncing our big girl in his other arm.

"Good morning my babies. Breakfast will be done in a few minutes." He takes her to her highchair since she has started to eat solid food more often. I had to put some in her milk starting at three months along with the occasional oatmeal scoops so she would actually be full and sleep through the night. Right as I'm getting ready to plate the food our big kids start to walk into the kitchen and sit at our large breakfast table.

"Good morning ma, dad, and there goes my baby." Darius greets us after giving me my morning kiss on the cheek and our girls follow suit. We have a nice breakfast of course the kids have their normal bickering here and there but for the most part we get along as a family like it was always meant to be us. Darius our oldest at fifteen likes to keep his siblings in check since he was so used to being their keeper when Myra was still alive but we have lessened his responsibilities in that area greatly so he can enjoy being a teenager. Denise and Myla, our twin pre-teens, are constantly using their twin powers as I like to call them to aggravate Darius, but we have started to keep them busy in gymnastics to help burn off some of that energy. Finally, the second baby of the group is our Mercy who is only eight and the quietest out of the bunch. She is much like Meira and I and loves her a good book. Dean made sure to include a large library for the both of us upstairs. The room has ten-foot-tall ceilings, and the bookshelves reach that high with two on three of the four walls as one wall has tall windows with a long comfy bench built into it. She has an entire wall for her books and my girl switches between them and her kindle. I am probably going to spend some time up there today while baby Delia is with the nannies, they are having a picnic outside in the back of the main house. Dean cleans up the kitchen while I get Delia dressed for her play time. I let Darius do it the other day and the twins the day after, but I don't want them to think it's their job to always do. I want them to enjoy their little sister not feel like she's another chore. So far it has worked but I still check in with them to make sure they feel like they get enough time with her and us. Dean enters Delia's room and smacks me on the ass inciting a laugh.

"Look at that ass jiggle, damn." He groans with his eyes still trained on my back side as I put on a light sweater.

"You don't have to go into the office today, right?" I question him as I strap her in her walker.

"No, I don't. You have something better in mind I can do with my time?" He comes up behind me rubbing his already hard dick against my back.

"Yes, I do. I was never able to give you your punishment the other day for keeping shit from me so be naked in the middle of our bed when I get back sir." I demand as I sashay out of the room putting a little more umph in my step.

"As you command my queen." I just shake me head at his antics and continue my walk to the house. I enter through the side entrance and I see my other three loves dropping the triplets off as well.

"Good morning Suga." Monty greets me first giving me a kiss on the top of the head once I reach close enough to them. Meira gives me our morning kiss and Jax gives me a hug and kiss on the forehead. I truly love our dynamic that we have built with each other. Everybody has their life partner but then we have each other as well so to say there is never a dull moment. I chat with them for a bit, but I have a certain chocolate man waiting on me that deserves to be punished.

"Good boy." I praise him when I walk into our room to find him lying on his back naked as the day he was born.

I walk into our large walk-in closet to the very back and grab our kink box. I decide to grab the ropes for his hands and feet, my bullet, blindfold, and the ball gag. He will learn about playing with me. I strip down to my birthday suit and walk back out to find him still in position.

"You being a good boy now won't lessen your punishment, but it is appreciated." I place everything on the bed then get to work tying his legs to each of the bed post using the single column tie he taught me and do the same thing to his arms. He is getting so turned on all nine inches he carries is standing up at attention. I blindfold him next then strap the ball gag around his head and I notice the pre cum leaking from his head. I lean over it and lick it all up.

"Mhmm." He moans through the ball gag. I grab the bullet, turning it on medium, rubbing it up his sides then up the middle of his chest, and around his nipples inciting another moan with a twist of his hips. I straddle his face rubbing my wet pussy across his mouth then over his nose back to his mouth and rubbing the bullet against my clit. The ball gags has holes in it but smooth so he will be able to taste my juices, but he won't be able to lick like I know he wants to. I start rocking back and forth as the bullets vibrations begin to push me closer to my orgasm. Throwing my head back moaning loud as the tingles start at my toes then up my spine.

"Mhmm fuck. You taste that baby?" I question him as I can feel my cum rubbing all over his mouth and leaking through the gag. I lift up and move back just a bit as I feel myself about to cum hard as fuck. I end up squirting all over his chin mouth some even wet the blindfold, so I sit on his chest then lean forward licking my juices from his face taking the blindfold off at the same time.

"Oh don't think your punishment is over." I assure him as I slid my pussy down his chest, over his stomach then liftin over his hard dick but not sitting on it but on his thighs. He has some pre cum that's built up again and I lick him clean then I get in a squat position with my feet flat on the bed and slide down his third leg slowly.

"Now you better not cum until I tell you to or I will stop longer each time, understand?" He nods his response, and I almost give in at the eagerness to please me look in his eyes, but I continue his punishment. I lift halfway and twerk on the head of his dick clenching as I rise. I drop allowing him to fill me completely and I feel the moment his balls draw up.

"You better not cum." I demand slapping him across the face then sliding off him completely bending over with my hands on his chest. He groans and I see his eyes roll on the back of his head. I slowly lower myself and just bounce up and down until my nut washes over me. I feel him draw up again and I stop. He yanks at the ropes, and I hear the post on the bed squeak from his strength.

"You better the fuck not Dean." I command him and he stops pulling at them. Since he wants to act up, I'm about to make it even worse for him. I get up and turn around getting on my knees and grabbing his ankles then bouncing my ass up and down. The air in the room is so thick with lust its almost overwhelming. I look back as I sit up and start rocking my hips back and forth. I see the moment his eyes roll in the back of his head this time because I am clenching around his thick length and my juices are sliding over his balls; I am so wet. I want to hear him beg so I turn just enough to release the ball gag.

"Fuck Sweetness please let me cum." He begs in his deep hoarse voice.

"I don't think you've learned your lesson yet." I come back with as I start to wind my hips while he's so deep it like he's in my damn stomach.

"Ooooh shit baby I promise I have. Fuck just like that." He moans.

"So, you promise to never hold anything back or lie to me?" I question as I am still winding my hips.

"Yes... Fuck yes Sweetness. Mhmm baby please... pleasssseee." He promises and I feel him tense as he's trying not to buck his hips.

"Cum D." I command when I start to bounce on his dick again and within a couple rise and falls of my hips, he's painting my walls with his cum.

"Fuck Sweetness." He groans. He turns his head to the side, and I watch over my shoulder as his chest rises and falls as he tries to catch his breath. We lay there for a few minutes then I lean forward to untie his legs then get up to untie his hands and the moment I get his last one he pounces on me like a damn lion.

"I really am sorry baby but don't think I'm done with you yet. You just had me tied up for almost an hour, you are going to take the rest of this nut Sweetness." He declares and proceeds to fuck me every way but wrong.

Chapter Nine

Dean Fredericks

It's been a quiet week since wifey put it on me something fierce. I'm over in our gym playing basketball with my brothers after a much-needed workout, I feel like I've been slacking. The building we designated for fitness was quick to put together but everything in here took months to collect due to the need for specific equipment for our future NFL players and the ladies requested a sauna as well as a hydro message bed for after workout recovery. It even has a dance room and mini gymnastics setup for our babygirls.

"So D, Kelia really tied you to the bed and edged you for a whole damn hour?" Chase asks me as we all gather on one of the benches on the left of the gym.

"Mannnn yes, the fuck she did. That woman tied my ass to the bed, blindfolded me, and put a damn ball gag in my mouth." I explain to him as the flashbacks cause chills to go from my spine right to dick.

"She told Meira she used ya face as her personal cum seat." Jax chuckles and shakes his head. Sometimes I hate that we are all so damn close cause the fuck nigga, shut up.

"Nigga nobody asked you but yes, she did. I am never holding shit back from that woman again. Had to fuck her for another forty-five minutes or so to feel satisfied.

Nuts still didn't feel empty enough." We all laughed at that point.

"So, has she decided what were doing about the counselors from the camp she was at? I know it's still on pause for her people." Meech questions from the other end of the bench.

"Oh, yea she wants to hunt each one of their asses down, but she is still contemplating what she wants to do with them exactly, but she wants it to be slow. Now as far as her parents she hasn't made up her mind but that sister of hers she requested Marsh and Bree on her. Find every bit of dirt you can find and air it all piece by piece. She wants her life completely ruined by the time she goes for her." I give them the instructions I was given this morning after breakfast.

"Say less and it sounds like all the crazy is starting to rub off or wake up those sides of her." Marsh states grabbing his towel to wipe his face and then I shake my head at the big ass tat around his throat of Bree's full name he got on their wedding night. These two decided they weren't going to wait at all and went to the courthouse then we all took a trip to the Bahamas. That was some of the cleanest beaches I've seen in a while. We never saw the reason to travel before our family started to grow like this but now every chance we get, we are taking the ladies or the entire family somewhere new. We all get up and part ways to our homes. It's still a lot of construction going on. The pool behind the main house isn't done, Marsh, Meech, Money, and Tru's homes are still in the works, but Chase's just finished about a month ago, so they recently moved out of the main house. We are all hoping those two stay together at this point with how funny Kenya keeps moving. When I enter my home the first thing I hear is my wife screaming for someone to get the fuck out causing my whole body to go on full alert. I quietly drop my gym bag then ease into my office off the foyer and grab one of my guns out the safe. I finally hear whomever she is arguing with.

"We came for our granddaughter, so stop with the dramatic Kelia. Have that man's children bring her down." A voice I recognize as her mother's demand her to do but she just repeats what she has been saying since I walked in. I keep my gun at my side and make myself known in our kitchen by sliding open the hidden door I installed, which is just one of many throughout the forty- eight hundred sq ft home.

"How the hell did you two get on our property and why haven't you called security Sweetness."

"We have a right to be here our granddaughter is here." Her father puffs out his chest, clearly forgetting the hand that was around his throat just over a month ago.

"You're right let me get them on the line to escort their asses outta here. I was just so damn shocked to even see them." She explains as she's opening the app on her phone to alert security while I move to stand next to her. I am absolutely seething at the fact they were able to gain access to our home without my knowledge; somebody is catching a bullet. I alert my brothers through our watch and the whole family with mom dukes leading the pack. The security guards come in a minute later looking confused as to why they have been summoned.

"Escort these fake ass Christians out of our family compound NOW and don't ever let them back in here." Moms shouts coming to stand next to Kelia and pulling her into a hug then rubbing her back.

"Wait I want to know why the fuck you let them onto our property without notifying any of us first." I question them as they move to stand behind them.

"Sir we were told they were Mrs. Kelia parents and just surprising her with a visit. We verified they were who they said and escorted them directly here." The guard named Ray spoke up first just sounding full of excuses because he knew the rules.

"That doesn't make a damn difference you know all guest at the gate need to be screened as well as an alert of their presence needs to be sent through the system. I don't give a fuck if they were the president and his funky ass wife the rules are there for a reason. Now you have traumatized Suga with their presence in her own home."

Monty's voice booms throughout the first floor as he scolds Ray.

"You all are some ungodly creatures, and you will not keep us away from our granddaughter since our child thinks she is above us. You raised these heathens, are you proud of yourself?" They have the audacity to question my mother's parenting and that caused her to come across Mrs. Black face with an open hand slap that left her red handprint displayed on the left side of her face. Mr. Black acts like he's about to move towards our mom and Jax has him by the throat and throws him against a nearby wall before he can even blink twice.

"I'm sorry Suga." He apologizes. He just reacted and didn't think about who he was actually grabbing.

"Nope don't be Smooth. He was going for mama Fredericks." She reassures him as she's walking over to him to wrap her arms around his waist for a hug then she pouts her lips to give her a kiss, and he obliges. She comes back to my side, and we interlock our hands as she rests her head on my arm.

"Get this trash off our family compound. Tru go with them and make sure Ray brings his ass back here."

"With pleasure bru." Tru responds as Ray helps Mr. Black off the floor and the other guard grabs Mrs. Black by the arm walking towards the front door.

"Unhand me you ape. This is not the end. We will get our grandbaby." Mrs. Black shouts as she is trying to wiggle her arm out his grip. They all exit and I take my wife aside to check in with her.

"Are you ok my Sweetness?" I place either of my hands on the side of her face after moving a long piece of hair behind her right ear. The shocked look on her face took me back to the night we first night we played predator and prey she was scared shitless when I came out with my real blade. Once she realized I wouldn't hurt her past her enjoyment but I never wanted to see the scared look again.

"Yes, I'm ok baby. I was just so shocked to see them and if I'm honest a little scared that they could find me. I never gave them this address before." She expresses rubbing her cheek against the inside of my palm and I pull her into me.

"I know that look arakunrin, your wheels are turning." Chase comes over to check on us.

"We will talk later take Iya home and make her that THC tea so she can calm her nerves before it's more bodies than necessary we have to get rid of." I instruct him and he simply nods his head then goes to do exactly what I told him to do. See most think that the psychopathic tendencies we all have came from our baba because of what he did but they actually come from our Iya that woman is nothing to be played with. She decided to go the route of playing normal instead of how she raised us which is to be who we are but learn certain things for our benefit. That THC tea should calm her enough to take an afternoon nap and then we can have a level-headed meeting with the rest of the fam later. In the meantime, however we are going to deal with Ray Lloyds dumb ass, so I hop on my golfcart and head towards the large shed we built near the trees Meira likes to put niggas in the woodchipper in front of. Once I arrive I see all my brothers except Chase waiting outside and I wonder what these fools are up to.

"So, we have a surprise for you." Monty informs me when I walk up, and I know this is about to be some shit. When we walk in these fools have a whole long ass dunk tank set up in the middle of the vast open area that has smaller rooms line up to the right. When I get close enough, I see a tied-up Ray sitting in the dunk seat and in the water below are damn alligators. I just shake my head because when the hell did these fools get time to build this shit one and two where the fuck did, they get the damn alligators in the water.

"Um who bright ass idea was this?" I question.

"The new addition to the family over there Tru." Meech discloses while pointing at a grinning Tru standing proudly next to his contraption and it just lets me know further, he was meant to be apart of the chaotic family.

"So how does this contraption work Tru?" I inquire as I walk up closer to admire his handy work.

"Just like any regular dunk tank with the exception that the target you must hit moves and so does the person you are dunking." He explains walking around to the front to stand next to me.

"Well get it started up arakunrin. You should've remembered to follow the fuckin rules instead of doing what you wanted." I remind him as Tru walks around the back to plug something in and the tank comes to life with the target moving along with a Ray in the seat. He is trying to stay perfectly still but in a moment it won't matter.

"Go ahead and have fun bru." Tru says while placing a small table next to me that has a basket full of baseballs.

"How about we have a little competition brothers. Hundred bucks to the person that dunks him first cause frankly I don't think he's going to last long even if those aren't adult gators in there." I offer and they all agree. We all take one throw turns with none of us hitting the moving target but it's my turn again and this fool is going in this time.

"Ight fellas get ready to pay up." I announce as I am gearing up to through the ball and shout yes the moment it connects with the target. Ray drops into the water screaming and struggling to get up as the six gators swim in for the kill. They all start biting on different parts of his body and attempting to do their infamous death roll but somehow, he gets his hands free to fight them off and reach for the chair that's reset itself. Surprisingly enough he's able to get away from them and pull himself back up into the seat since it's the only place he can go, Tru made sure of that with the razor-sharp edges all around the tank.

"Damn he actually go out. Ok new bet. I bet two hunnid he won't last the next two dunks." Jax declares and we all start placing bets on different amounts. I end up agreeing with Jax since the bites on his body don't look too severe and due to the fact, he's a decently large man. I have to chuckle for a moment because seeing him sitting there on only his boxers shaking like a sinner in church and drenched from head to toe is too funny. Jax is up next and he dunks his ass quick but this time he reaches for the edge of the tank like the frantic idiot he is. He slices his hand open initiating a stream of blood from both to slide down the outside and inside of the tank. The gators go wild biting at him and I see the moment they take a chunk out of his calf. Ray manages to get back to the chair with a large piece of his calf missing so much so we can see a piece of bone sticking through the fatty tissue. He also has deep bite wounds to his left arm and his hip. Chase goes next and lands his hit as well but the gators must be ready to really eat because one goes for his neck this time around.

"Ight niggas pay up." I demand as the tank goes from clear water that's just tinted by blood to the entire thing turning crimson red and we no longer hear his cries for help.

"Ah hell how are we going to explain this one?" Chase questions.

"That nigga only had an elderly mom with Alzheimer's in a nursing home and some little jump off so, nobody will miss him and I'll make sure the nursing home keeps getting paid." I inform them as we all stand around now passing a joint around.

"Naw don't worry about it I'll just buy it under one of the LLC's we have." Meech decides and I just shrug my shoulders as that is perfectly fine with me, more income.

"But what the hell are we doing with those niggas?" Jax questions blowing smoke out his nose then passing me the blunt and I was wondering the same thing because it better not be our pond on the other side of our land.

"Oh, I can have them shipped off in the morning to the Everglades." Tru advises us and once the blunt is out we all head back to the main house.

"Naw keep them for a bit my wife may want to drop someone in there. They make cleanup easy." Monty states and we all agree then head our separate ways.

Chapter Ten

Kelia Fredericks

We're all sitting in the family room awaiting Meira, Jax, and Monty to finish putting the triplets down.

"You feeling ok my Sweetness?"

"Yes, baby I am good." I answer him as I rub my face against his arm that I have my arms wrapped around while his hand rest on my thigh. After a few minutes they all come down stairs to join us coming through one of the secret doors in the family room by the large fireplace. The door is so seamless if you don't know its there you would never find it.

"Aight let's deal with this family business." Monty states sitting in their custom lazy boy chair that fits the three of them perfectly.

"Before we get into handling new business, I need to tell you about some old business our lil brothers decided to handle for us." Dean states looking over at Chase and them.

"What's up arakunrin?" Jax asks with his hand resting on Meira's thigh.

"Well Chase, Money, and Tru along with Meech took it upon themselves to knock Calder off the board, permanently." He informs us all and I see Meira eyes light up then her head pops up from Monty's shoulder.

"Wait you sure he's gone?" Monty questions his brothers.

"Yes, I didn't say anything earlier but I kinda took a souvenir when the boys weren't looking and have been wanting to give it to you Meira." Money states he looking nervous.

"I like souvenirs Money. What is it?" Meira sits up completely looking like a kid in the toy store. Money gets up pulling out a velvet box from his pocket then drops to his knees but before he can open the box Monty and Jax are on his ass.

"Aight nigga you arakunrin but don't get fucked up." Jax threatens and we all laugh when Meira hits him in the stomach.

"Stop it you two. Open the box Money." Meira demands and he does as he is told. He reveals a severed white man's finger that has a large ring on it.

"Nigga when did you go back and get the fools finger?" Chase questions as he looks over to see what's in the box.

"When you guys were walking around the back to make sure no one was coming out after we set the fire." He explains and clearly everyone recognizes the ring to know it's his. He goes to stand but Meira pulls him in for a heated kiss and we hear him moan.

"Thank Money. Thank you, Chase, Tru, and Meech too."
They nod their heads, and Money starts to get up to walk
back to his seat as he's biting his bottom lip.

"So, Bree has already located some crazy shit on ya fam
Ke. Do you want to hear it?" Marsh checks with me
before continuing and I nod my head yes because I'm
ready to deal with all of their asses now.

"Well turns out ya brother-in-law is cheating because ya
sister can't have kids, at least that's what we guess. We
also believe that's why your parents are going so hard
about gaining access to baby Delia." Bree details
looking at me with concern in her eyes before she goes
on.

"Guys listen I am ok, and I am ready to complete my
healing by destroying all of them one by one." I convey
my feelings with all the strength they are all giving me to
move forward.

"That's all we needed to know Ke, we got you. So, we
located all the counselors from the camp. Two of them
live in Georgia, three are in KC, and one is in Michigan
living off the grid so he may be a bit harder to get ahold
of." Chase fills us in.

"Well, here's what I want for them, bring them all to KC. I
always wanted to see the wolves you have baby and
that darn wax museum you have Monty bear or you guys
can surprise me by creating something just for me." I

express my wants to them and I see the moment they all agree to do whatever I need.

"Sounds like our Suga wants to have some fun y'all." Monty says with this sinister grin on his face that would probably scare the average woman but is turning me the fuck on right now.

"Oh one last thing brother-in-law has a whole family in Cali. What you wanna do about them?" Bree adds in as I'm sure she notices the shift in my energy and Dean squeezes my thigh as he does.

"I want you to rip that bitches life apart like she did mines all those years ago. Start with delivering the photos of his family to the other family as well as the whole congregation and send their official marriage license, address, and whatever photos of her and him to the other woman too. After that just keep someone on her and get whatever dirt you can find on her specifically. I just know she's not squeaky clean." I instruct them. Mama Fredericks gives me a kiss on the cheek then goes to the other side of the house to her room then I give Dean a kiss and he nods giving me permission to do as I please. I get up then walk over to Monty and straddle his lap. He places his hands on either ass cheek and squeezes.

"What do you need Suga?" He questions after he takes one of his hands off my ass then wraps it around my neck rubbing his thumb over my pulse.

"I need you to take me upstairs, put me in the swing, lick and fuck me with that sexy evil grin you have going on right now." I lay my head on his chest and turn my head towards Meira who gives me a kiss then goes to slide onto Jax's lap reverse cow girl with her legs spread open as she looks at Dean.

"Whatever you need Suga." He declares while he stands with me still wrapped around him and heads over to the hidden door. The family follows except Tru and Money and I realize they rarely ever do but the one time they did they only watched. We barely make it upstairs to the room before Monty pins me to the wall and wraps my legs around his neck licking my clit through my thin lace thong.

"Mhmm shi... shit." I can't help but moan and rub my pussy over his lips. I hear other moans coming from my left and see Meira leaned against the wall with one leg over Jax's shoulder as he sucks and licks her soul from her pussy.

"Fuck Monty bear I'm... I'm cumming." I stutter out as I feel my cum slide down his tongue that's flat against my pussy the tip of it licking at my entrance and the base rubbing against my clit with him moving it side to side.

"Nut one down and so many more to go my Suga." He growls after kissing my pussy then bringing me back down to wrap my legs around his waist then tonguing my mouth the way he just did my pussy. I moan into his mouth tasting myself on his tongue and all over his juicy lips. We all finally make it to the Sinful Sanctuary and he does exactly what I need. The next morning after hanging out with the kids since it's the weekend they all head to their rooms and Delia goes down for a nap. I am waiting on Marsh and Bree to come over since they texted to let me know they have found something I am going to want to see immediately. I hear Dean coming downstairs after making sure Delia was truly asleep. A knock comes on the door then I hear the beep of the locks opening.

"Hi Ke." They both greet me and give me a kiss on either cheek while I sit in my favorite black oversized swivel accent chair. They take a seat in the loveseat across from me as Dean sits next to me after giving Bree a kiss on the cheek and dapping Marsh.

"So what's up arakunrin kekere?" Dean questions.

"So, look you told us to keep digging on your sister, so we hacked her phone, and you won't believe the shit we found. Also Money was able to burn down the camp and relocate the kids that didn't want to go back to their families." Bree informs us. I don't understand why any of them would want to go back to parents when given the option to go elsewhere but I nod for her to continue about my sister. I am just glad that place is closed for good.

"Man, this woman has had like three abortions because she doesn't know who the father was since ha ass cheating with two different men. She is the one who put the idea in your parent's head to get Delia so she can raise her as her own. They are trying to find a way to label y'all as incompetent parents. Man, yo family is triflin as fuck." She finishes and I can't believe I actually called these muthafucka's family.

"They aren't my family. So go ahead and start the recking ball just as I told you the last time." I get up and start for the stairs because I need a moment to myself. Like I knew my family wasn't much of shit after being sent to the damn conversion camp but the whole plotting to take my child is wild. I walk upstairs then go into my meditation closet and lock my door even though if Dean wants to get to me, it won't stop him one bit. He understands I need space but will never allow me to wallow in my feelings to long and I love that he doesn't just take care of my physical, finances, but my mental above all.

Chapter Eleven

Dean Fredericks

It's been about two weeks since we put the wife's plan in the action and to say our days have been entertaining is putting it mildly. I did have to give her some time to herself after Bree revealed everything. I know it must be hard to realize you have to cut off your entire family. I can't imagine life without my brothers or my mother for that matter. We are currently taking a break from building Meech's home, and I can feel the tension rolling off this Chase.

"Arakunrin what's going on?" I question on him as we sit on one of the wooden benches the women insisted on having spread through out the walkways to each home.

"Man, I think Kenya is cheating on me." He drops the bombshell none of us were expecting. I have to laugh for a moment before responding because Meech almost chokes on his sports drink.

"What the hell makes you think some crazy shit like that?" Jax beats me to asking him.

"Besides the fact that we're the only engaged couple in the group and haven't even set the date for our wedding. She's been whispering on the phone and leaving the room when taking calls from someone. Then the other day she came up missing for hours and never answered my calls." He gets increasingly pissed the more he recalls all the odd things she has been doing lately. I must admit that her behavior does sound suspicious.

"Do you want us to look into what the hell is going on with her?" I question.

"Or I can sick Meira on her. You know she will get the truth out of her." Monty offers and that may be the best idea but from the look on his face he's not going to choose that option not yet at least.

"No, I am going to let things play out for a while besides we need to make sure Ke finishes her healing process properly. Did y'all see the latest text from your plant at the church?" He changes the subject, and we catch the hint.

"Yea that shit was funny as hell. Wifey and I watched the video on the tv like it was a damn movie." I inform him as I start to laugh again and so do they. On Tuesday we received the video of her sisters' husband mistress showing up at the church raising hell. She ends up jumping on Kelia's sister and snatching her wig off. I slid off the couch onto the floor when she called her a patchy head, dry pussy, forty years a slave smelling, possum faced ass bitch. We expected her to turn up when we found out how young she was and that he had proposed to her with the same ring he gave Kelia's sister, which of course we told her about. What we did not expect was when she finished showing out at the church that she would leave the two-month-old baby they had together behind with signed papers signing over her rights. The broad kept the ring though and we all figured she was going to pawn it. After a few more minutes we got back to work.

"Well things are really coming together in here." Meira walks up and stands in the doorway to admire the work we've done. The house base plus outer walls went up months ago when Meech finally decided on the square footage of four thousand square feet. We just finished the last bit of the framework just now.

"Everything good my Phoenix?" Jax questions as he makes it to her first then gives her a kiss on the cheek.

"Outside of you six missing dinner with the family, yes everything is good." She looked at each of us with a frown on her face then we all look at our watches and started apologizing. We had our music going and were just in a groove.

"I'm so sorry Ife mi time just got away from us." Monty apologizes again as he pulls her into his arms and kisses the top of her head.

"Alls forgiving. I know you guys get into your groove and I know Meech is ready for his place to be done. Oh, by the way Chase tell your woman stop avoiding me before she pisses me off. You two it's time to put the kids to bed and then I have an early flight in the morning." She commands my brothers and in the same breath warns Chase about Kenya. A part of me knew Meira would catch on to her sketchy behavior before Chase decided on what he wanted to do. Chase just nods his head as he clearly retreats into his thoughts as he starts to go next door to his home and the three of them make their way across the walkway to the main house.

"Chase you may have to deal with that sooner rather than later because if she pisses off La'Meira shit is going to go left." I shake his shoulder to get him to really hear what I'm telling him.

"For real arakunrin. You know the moment Meira gets fired up then Bree and Ke jumping with her." Marsh drives home my point further. I honestly don't believe she's cheating but she is definitely hiding something from the family and either way it's going to cause a big problem if not dealt with.

"Ibi aabo mi." Kelia calls for me at the door and I swear since i have been teaching her differnet phrases in our native language she has become even more fuxking sexy. She picks up anything quickly and this has been no differnet. When she came to me and said the phrase it took me a moment to know what it meant but once i did i reminded her that i'd always be her safe place. I dap my brother up and head out with my woman.

"The kids wanted alone time with their baby sister so they went own ahead to get ready for bed. I figured we could have some alone time in the hot tub once you get cleaned up and eat your dinner."

"Sounds good to me Sweetness." I express wrapping one arm around her waist then leaning over to kiss the top of her head and we take our peaceful walk across the walkway to our home. I take me a nice warm shower making sure to scrub a bit more in certain areas since a nigga been sweating all day. I don't take to long though cause a brothers stomach is growling and I am ready to be balls deep in my woman, which is why i skip the boxers and just slide on my basketball shorts. I head downstairs and grab my plate out the microwave then dig in until i hear our favorite song playing through the outside speakers on low. I scarf down the rest of my food and wash it down with a shot of Jacks then head out the door.

"That's how you feel my sweetness?" I whisper in her ear once I walk up behind her in the hot tub and she turns to show me exactly what time shes on. She pulls down my basketball shorts revealing my deep v cut then keeps pushing them down until she's face to face with my long, thick chocolate dick. Without using her hands she lick around the head and slowly suck me into her warm invitng mouth.

"Oooh fuck Sweetness. That's my girl hmmm just like that." I moan as I start to fuck her mouth. Slowly I thrust my hips forward gliding my dick against her wet tongue and bumping against the back of her throat. I grab Ke's head to hold her in place as it begins to feel so fucking good then my thrust get faster and the saliva starts sliding down the sides of her mouth.

"Fuck mo nife enu re." I growl inciting her own moan around my dick that made her throat vibrate. She creates suction and grabs my dick at the base then begins stroking it with a twist. I have to release her head and grab those juicy tits then rub circles around her dime sized hard erected nipples. The mixture of the heat from the hot tub, low music, and the flames from the torches mixed with the energy radiating off both our bodies has me feeling so intoxicated. I curse and tell her some more about loving her and that mouth before i shoot cum down her throat. I slowly pull out of Kelia's mouth and lean over to give her a kiss before joining her in the hot bubbles.

Chapter Twelve

La'Meira Fredericks

"Babe we are going to be fine. Money has our backs, and you know how I move." I attempt to assure both my big crazy ass men but these fools not budging much.

"Money you always stay by their sides and keep your head on a swivel. I mean it nigga you have precious cargo in your hands." Jax instructs him with a bit of underline threat, and I just shake my head at their antics.

"Man fuck this I'm going with y'all. Jax and Dean can handle the other two." Monty declares as he grabs me up in his arms.

"Big daddy relax you have my location at all times and you guys won't be far from us with the jet on standby. Besides, you guys don't leave until tonight for Michigan and y'all will be on the way right after. I will be in bed waiting on you." I finally convince him to relax, and we board the jet to KC. We have three targets to get at in KC but they are fairly easy targets from the info the guys have gathered thus far. I planted a bug in their devices a week ago to get a read on their habits and as soon as we land there is one I'm picking up at a coffee shop near their home. I still can't believe these fools are walking around freely after all the sick shit they did to children in their care but I guess I shouldn't be surprised.

"Ok Meira here's the syringes with the serum Meech created to make them sick and then collapse. These should be smooth captures, drop em off at his lab, then off to Monty's crib." Money recites the plan to me but more so himself. I get it he's nervous with Mama Fredericks and I in his care.

"It's going to be fine Money trust me." I assure him then grab his hand to lay it on my thigh and rub circles on top of it to calm him.

"What they say about you is right." He says finally relaxing and leaning his head back with his eyes closed.

"What do they say about me?" I question him.

"You have some type of magic powers or something going on. You calm us so easily, it's almost scary." He fills me in on the talk in the family and I just giggle because it's not the first time one of them have said that.

"I just like my family at peace and you are apart of the family now so you need me I got you. You never got a chance to tell me how you liked your gift before I went into labor." I continue rubbing circles between his thumb and pointer finger, occasionally applying pressure.

"That gift was much appreciated. That's why it was a must to grab you that souvenir. I haven't had many people around me do something for me that didn't want shit back." He explains still leaned back with his eyes close and his breathing even.

"I figured as much but you don't have to worry about that anymore. I was just glad I could deliver those backstabbing crouch goblins but no more of that relax we have work to get to the moment we land." He does as I instruct him, and I check on mom who decided to sit behind us, but she is fast asleep. I sit back down and close my eyes for a few myself. When I get comfortable, I feel Money's hand back on my thigh and I wait to see what he's going to do but he keeps it in the same spot, so I just place my hand on top of his then nod off. Soon I feel him squeezing my thigh and calling my name to wake me.

"Aight let's get this dealt with." I state once we step off the jet.

"I think we need to split up baby girl. These are easy targets, and I want to get this all over with so I can get back to all my grandbabies." Valerie tries to convince me but there is no chance in hell we are splitting up.

"Mama, I agree they are easy targets, but we can't split up. We don't need to take unnecessary risks when we have no reason to rush. Besides your sons would blow a gasket if they knew we did, and I can't shut down the cameras in all three locations at the same time." We load up in the truck and she finally drops the subject. I pull up the trackers on my laptop and the first target is exactly where she should be at this time. I advise Money on where to go, and we head there in a comfortable silence. Of course, I get a text from my men checking on us as if they can't see my location and damn vitals for that matter. Just as I thought getting our targets were a piece of cake. We just dropped them off to Meech's lab and are stopping by Mama Fredericks home first because she wanted to grab a few things. When we pull up to the house I notice a man leaning on a newer model Cadi dressed real sharp and I hear Mama Fredericks kiss her teeth in the backseat which let me know she knew him at least.

"Y'all gone on in the house I'll deal with him." She directs us as we hop out the truck.

"Naw I'll stay right here I don't like this nigga." Money announces as he leans back against the railing on her porch with his arms crossed and I move to sit in one of the chairs she has setup because I'm getting a bad feeling from him as well.

"Fine but I got this." She says and walks off to him. The moment she gets close to him they break out into an argument and It takes a lot for me not to jump on his ass. I hear vehicles speeding down the long driveway and I see the moment he reaches for her but she jumps back away from him. The tires of about three trucks screech to a halt in the driveway and Money pulls his weapon with one while pulling Mama Fredericks behind him with his other hand. I stand at the top of the stairs with my gun drawn, ready for whatever is about to pop off.

"Ahh so I can kill two birds with one stone. I am definitely getting paid double for this. Look you can come the easy way or the hard way either you two are coming with me." One of the pale faced but seemingly well-dressed men that hopped out one of the trucks announces. I count about fifteen of them and they clearly have underestimated us.

"You slimy snake you set me up!" Mama Fredericks yells over Money's shoulder as he backs her up the stairs towards me.

"Look you been playing games cause of these grown ass sons of yours and they were paying a lot of money to get at you, so it was an easy sell." The dude I now realize is the boyfriend Monty told me about a while back, but we all thought they broke up.

"You are going to regret crossing me, Frank." She states through gritted teeth her voice laced with venom and I hear her mumble her baby was right about him then she shakes her head.

"Last chance buddy, just hand them over and we will let you live." Pale face states dropping his voice an octave like he's scaring somebody, so I show him who he's messing with and send off two shots his way. The first hits the man to his right and the other hits the man behind him. Mama Fredericks fires her weapon next after coming from behind Money hitting her ex-boo square between the eyes and a laugh at the look on the pale face dudes as more bodies drop when Money starts ringing off shot after shot. The pale face takes cover behind his truck with the few men he has left and starts sending shots our way. I don't notice one of them shooting from one of the other trucks and Money moves quickly to stand in front of me, blocking me from the shot but getting hit himself. He stumbles for a moment but sends shots back and kills the dude. I see the blood that's quickly dripping from his shoulder and as I grab him, I notice the shot to his side as well. I motion for Mama Fredericks to get the door open as we back up into the house still firing and dodging shots. Money was holding on strong until we got in the house then he fell to his knees and coughed up blood on the floor.

"The boys reinforced the entire house with bullet proof glass and doors after what happened last year. They aren't getting in here." Valerie announces and it gives me some solace until Money falls over on his back and I see just how bad his wounds are.

"Ma help me get him on the table." Money sits up on the floor in visible pain but trying to save face. I have him wrap one his arm over each of our shoulders and we walk his large ass over to the table. Money is not as big as my men but he's still standing at least six foot two and running at about two hundred pounds but he's a good looking man with his honey skin and toned body.

We finally get him on the table laying flat so I can look over his wounds.

"Ma they should have put a few of my emergency medical bags around here can you grab one of them." I request as I rip off Money's black t-shirt and start to really examine his wounds but before I can get to deep my phone rings and I already know who it is.

"What the heck is going on Ife mi? You and moms heart rate was just through the roof and I can't access her cameras." Monty comes roaring through the phone I laid next to Money when I put it on speaker.

"Bae I really don't have time to explain everything I'm trying to keep Money from dying on me." I shout. Ma comes back with one of my bags and I get to work. I have her take some gauze to apply pressure to the wound in his side while I get the IV set up on the other side.

"We are on the way Ife mi." He informs me and ends the call. I get a text from Jax and Dean to stay my ass inside and keep their little brother alive. I go back to the wound in his shoulder, and I am glad to find it was a through and through, but I noticed it nicked a nerve.

"Hey this was not the way I wanted to give you your chip, but I need your vitals, and I need you to stay with me. Your brothers are on the way. You did great now keep doing it and stay strong for us all." I get a weak nod of his head then I lean over and insert the chip into his right arm. His vitals come in on my watch within a few seconds and fuck they aren't looking good. I get him sewn, cleaned, then patched up and I start to notice his vitals rising. Only having local anesthetics to get him put back together had to have been hard on him. I realize I have a text and that makes me also notice I've been working on Money for a couple hours because then men have landed.

"Ok Money keep holding on your brothers are almost here." I assure him. The whole time I was working on him I could occasionally hear Mr. Pale face and his men trying to break down the doors after they realized the windows weren't breakable.

"Hey babygirl at some point a few more trucks showed up with tools. I was worried until I just heard you say the boys have landed. How's my other boy here doing?" She walks up to his side and rubs her hand over his hair then kisses him on the forehead. When the fellas told her they were adopting him as their brother she welcomed him and Tru as her sons with open arms. Money actually cried that night when she hugged him and we all know it's an even deeper story to our Money that we will get to hear one of these days. For now, we need to deal with these fucking idiots outside and the bastards that thought it was a good idea to make my Ke's life a living hell. I lean over to give Money a kiss on the lips, and I feel him kissing me back for a moment which incites a smile from me. I get another text from Jax letting me they were coming down Mama Fredericks long driveway.

"Ok Blake they're here love. You did great now just hold on so we can get you home." I hear gun fire going off and then tires screeching then pulling off. I think we are home free until I hear the alarm going off for Money's vitals on my watch.

"Shit Money... Moneyyyy."

Chapter Thirteen

Kelia Fredericks

Getting these idiots locked up in Meech's lab started out easily but with Money gone saying it has been hard is putting it mildly. Jax and Meech have been back and forth from Meech's lab for the past week to make sure the four we have there stay sedated. The asshole in Michigan put up a serious fight but he was no match for my Hubby and Chocolate Bear. Tonight, they are headed to Georgia to get the other two then dropping them off at the lab so I'm staying with Meira.

"Hi babe, you already know where I'm heading. You can hop in the bed if you want or come with." She tells me as I enter her and Monty's room but she's preparing to leave through one of the secret doors in the room. I decide to head down with her and walk through the hidden door then close it behind us. The walk down the hall is a quiet one, but we reach the room we are heading to and when she opens the door it reveals a sleeping Money. He coded twice, which caused Meira to revive him both times and I think that took a lot out of her. He has been doing better these past few days and stirs when he hears us fully enter the room.

"Well hello beautiful ladies." He greets us in his low gruffy voice and moves to sit up.

"Hi Blakey, how are you feeling today?" Meira greets him then leans down to kiss him on the cheek and I do the same on the other cheek.

"I'm feeling much better thanks to you Doc. Who knew all I had to do was get shot to get some attention from the women around here." He jokes as Meira checks his IV and vitals on her watch.

"Monty said he got you out of bed earlier to walk, how did it feel?" She questions him after sitting in the chair next to his bed and I sit on the arm of the chair.

"It felt good getting out of this bed its comfortable and all but I'm ready to get back to moving around." He responds directly to her gaze, with Meira being responsible for his presence in bed.

"Fine you can start moving around for a couple of hours a day no more Money. Your stitches should be close to dissolving but no lifting anything, bending over, or stretching your arms over your head." She gives him specific instructions, and he listens intently because he wants to get the hell out of this bed. We continue to sit with him, just talking for a bit more and she gives him the green light to go downstairs with the fellas while they pack. We all make our way to the elevator then head over to Monty and Jax's office.

"Hi my Phoenix and Suga." Jax greets us as he daps Money up then pulls both of us in for a hug and kisses the top of our heads. She walks over to Monty wrapping her arms around his neck from behind as he sits at his desk chair and I head over to Dean who's packing a duffle bag with guns and other equipment.

"So, any word on who attacked us at moms?" Meira questions them all. They found out a few days ago the dead ones that were left were hired mercenaries, but it's been a bitch trying to figure out who hired them. Meira has been fully focused on getting Money well, so she hasn't did her normal hack job yet.

"No but we figured out the white boy you described is a problem solver for politicians. We need you to do your magic to get his location so we can have a word with him quicker." Dean informs her as he wraps his arms around me from behind and kisses the top of my head. It always feels so warm and safe in his arms, it's like my own personal cocoon.

"Ok I'll get on it tonight. When exactly are you leaving?" Tonight, Monty, Jax, and Dean are heading out to Georgia but Marsh, Bree, and Meech are heading to KC to deal with my sister as well as check on the others. I can't wait to see the look on her face when they drop the bomb on all the abortions she's had and why at the church. Its was only right they do it there since one of the guys she's sleeping with turns out to be the pastor's married son. The one turned out to be a coworker at the clinic she works at and the other dude she apparently met at a club she had no business at. Bitch had three other niggas in rotation besides her husband.

"We leave in about an hour based on the bug you left on their devices they both will be at home soon and staying put for the night." Jax replies to her and the only thing I want to know is when they will be back because I hate sleeping without my man. I know I'll be up under my bae Meira but it's just not the same.

"Ok but when will y'all be back?" I ask.

"A couple days Sweetness. We have to make sure everything is clear. We've been covering our tracks, but we like to make sure we are really in the clear with the moves we're making. Plus, it will be time for you come over to start your healing soon, so we want to have your options prepared." Dean informs me as he turns me around to look him in the eyes.

"He's right and are you truly ready to begin this journey? Tearing your sister's life apart is one thing Suga but this part with them is different. It's going to take more outta ya." Jax questions as he comes up behind me then turns me around to face him and the others.

"Yes, I'm ready. I can't keep having this cloud holding over my head and I've tried traditional therapy, and it didn't help enough." I explain to them all.

"Ok then we're doing this." Jax declared and turned away to walk towards Meira then wrapped her up in his arms. We hung out with the guys until it was time for them to go. Chase helped Money get to bed while Meira and I went to get ready for bed ourselves. I strip while she gets the shower started since she prefers to shower before taking a bath. I get cleaned up first so I can start our bubble bath. By the time I'm getting in she is getting out of the shower she sits behind me, and I lean back with my back to her chest.

"This was just what I needed." She exhales as she picks some bubbles up and rubs them over my shoulders.

"Same here. These past few weeks have been stressful, tiring, and too damn eventful for my liking." I express then release a deep sigh. We lay in silence just rubbing bubbles on each other then she starts rubbing bubbles around both of my nipples and they go hard instantly. She applies pressure by squeezing them between her two fingers.

"Mhmm Meira." I moan as she starts to twist them slightly while still pinching them.

"I want you to rub that clit for me." She whispers in my ear and my hand moves at her demand. I start rubbing my clit then lean my head back as I bit on my bottom lip.

"Just like that babe." She moans in my ear then starts nibbling on my earlobe which is one of my sensitive spots and sends me over the edge.

"Mhmm yesssss." I moan as I am still rubbing circles over my clit and she continues pinching then twisting my nipples all while sucking on the sensitive spot on my neck. My release slowly washes over me and has my body tingling all over as if I was just zapped by a small voltage of electricity.

"Good girl now let's get to bed." She commands then kiss me on my neck and patting my sensitive bud under the water. We get rinsed off, dried, and handle our skin care routines. I always thought about women sexually but being around Meira like this makes me slightly wonder could it be more than sex. Meira leaves out the bathroom first and I follow behind her after a few minutes. When I enter the room I find her sitting on the edge of the bed with her legs spread and that fat pussy calling my name. I strut over to her and kneel in between her legs.

"As much as I want you to put those pretty lips on this pussy, tonight is about you. I need you to release some of that stress you are holding in your body. Go lay on your stomach." She commands me and I do as she says. She pulls out some body oil then drips it all over my body. She starts at my shoulders and works her way down to my feet. She has relaxed every last one of my muscles and when she has me turn over then starts the same routine I feel like I'm floating on a cloud.

"Fuck this feels amazing Meira." I say just above a whisper. When Meira finishes my massage she straddles my waist and leans forward to plant a soft kiss on my lips. I love the feel of her pillowy soft lips against mines. We break our kiss but she continues kissing down my neck then over my breast where she stops and curls her tongue around my nipple. She proceeds to suck my nipple between the same soft lips she kissed me with.

"Mhmm." I moan. She nibbles on it for a moment then soothing the sting with the tip her tongue then her lips again. She does the same thing to my other titty then makes her way down my stomach with soft and slow kisses. Meira has me so turned on I can already feel my juices sliding from my pussy onto to the bed. She places one kiss on my clit then moves and I lift my head to see what she's doing.

"Now it's time to really release the remaining stress babe. I'm about to my make you and this pussy cry, now lay back." Meira says inciting a shiver to take over my body. She leans over me with the dildo she pulled from the drawer and taps me on the chin with it.

"Open up." She orders and I do just that. Sucking on it like it's Dean fat chocolate dick instead. She removes it from my mouth then rubs it down my body until she reaches my pussy then pushes my legs to give her full control. Meira rubs the brown dildo between my pussy lips before pushing it into me. When she finds a rhythm, she leans forward then slides her tongue between my lips up to my clit and sucks it in between her lips. I feel her tongue rapidly flicking against my clit initiating the first of what I am sure will be many orgasms tonight. Meira doesn't let up, I feel the dildo so deep in my pussy in this position it feels like Dean is balls deep and trying to rearrange my guts. Her warm mouth and tongue continues it's assault on my pussy inciting another orgasm but this one hits me so hard tears fall from the corners of my eyes, my back arches off the bed, and before I realize it I'm squirting all over her face but she licks me right through it while I cream all over the dildo.

"Fuuucckk." I scream but she never lets up and another orgasms washes over me. The feeling of her warm tongue sliding across my clit and the in and out motion of that dildo is spinning crazy.

"You taste so fucking good Ke mhmm." She moans into my pussy. When she takes the dildo out then turn it on placing it on my clit I damn near jump out my skin and I cum instantly on her tongue that she's swirling around in my pussy. We have been going at it for at least thirty or forty-five minutes with her changing from doing both to just the dildo giving me slow then fast pumps and she is finally letting up.

"Damn." Is all I can get out as she trails kisses up my body then leaves and I suspect to the bathroom. My suspicions are confirmed when I hear the water running and she comes back placing a warm rag on my pussy.

"You look exhausted but satisfied. Just what I wanted now crawl over there and get some rest." She directs me then slides out the bed and before my eyes shut for good I hear water running again then a slight movement in the bed and I'm out like a light.

Chapter Fourteen

Dean Fredericks

"Well brother looks like our girls just finished having some fun." I tell them from the backseat of the truck we picked up from an old friend once we landed while looking at Kelia's heart rate calm and go into her restful rate. An unexperienced nigga would've thought something was wrong with how high her heart rate went but I know her pulse better than I know my own and that was definitely an orgasm hitting her hard as fuck.

"Trust, I noticed I've been monitoring Meira's heart rate since we left." Monty states from the front passenger seat and I can't help but to chuckle at us.

"Well that means she gave Suga the distraction and release she needed. You know Meira is always on it." Jax says from the driver's seat.

"That she is. I was thinking about putting together a couple's getaway trip in a couple weeks since it's been a lot of draining shit going on." I confess. I was thinking about doing it after everything is dealt with but getting a break in between bullshit may be better.

"Bet let's make it something tropical. The least amount of clothes the ladies have to wear and the most drinks and weed we can get into all of us the better without worry the better arakunrin." Monty didn't have to tell me that because that's exactly what I was looking into. We have made it to the first location and hopped out the truck to walk up to the front door like we own the place.

"So what about a guys trip afterwards? We haven't been out hunting in a while." I suggest as we enter the home like it belongs to us, using a key to open the door instead of picking the lock and now entering the pin code on the alarm.

"Man I'll think about it. We just got our woman back after four long fucking months." Jax says as he walks up the stairs with us right behind him.

"For real though." Monty adds as we step into the room and this old bitch is getting her back blown out by a nigga she probably paid.

"Yo who the fuck are y'all? Bitch I'm not into no funny shit." The young dude shouts hopping from the bed. I notice the gun on the bed side table and the look he just gave it but beat him to my weapon but chose to use the darts Meech made for us instead of a real bullet. Whatever Meech put in that damn thing was strong as hell cause that lil nigga slumped over quick as fuck then hit the floor.

"Whhho who are you? What do you want?" The old hag stutters over her words and I say old hag because of what the bitch did to my wife but she can't be any older than mid fifties.

"You should really learn to not judge people for who they are or what they like but whatever we will get to that later." Monty replies leaning against the doorframe with his normal wicked grin.

"Time to go night... night." I say right before shooting her with the tranquilizer. Jax moves to grab her out the bed then remembers she has on no clothes.

"Ugh damn bro couldn't you have made her dress her damn self-first." Jax complains visibly irritated by the fact he has to touch the chick. I help him get her dressed while Monty does the same for the young nigga but he wasn't fully naked thankfully. This big ass fool throws the dude over his shoulder like a lil rag doll then grabs all his stuff he can find and heads downstairs, I presume to his car. We get things cleaned up and head downstairs with her next. Thanks to the bestie all cameras on this block as well as the next few have been disabled plus the houses here aren't that close together and it's about two a.m. these old folk's sleep. We get her settled in the trunk and Monty dealt with old boy around the corner but made sure to give him something that would make him forget everything. We made our way to the next stop and thankfully this fool was asleep, so we snatched him quick and put him in the trunk. It's about five a.m. in the morning and to hear my phone ringing with the wife's name worried me since she usually sleeps until nine when the kids don't have school.

"Good morning, Sweetness, is everything ok?"

"Yes babe. I was just calling to let you guys know to put the bitches on ice and get home the twins and Darius birthday is next week. We are having a huge family cookout pool party since Meira threatened the pool guys to get it finished without any further delays. So we have a lot of work to do." I chuckled at my best friends antics.

"Got it wifey, I'll let my brothers know. I love you." I admitted because I'm missing my wife.

"I love you too. See you tomorrow." She expressed and ended the call.

"Ight fellas we are putting the niggas on ice we have the kids birthday next week and our lovely Meira has threatened the pool guys into making sure they're finished by next week in time for the party." They both nodded their agreement and we make it over to the airport to load up our deliveries then head to KC. Walking into Meech's lab we walk all the way to the back then through the double doors to the room he has setup like a coroner's morgue with rows of doors on the back wall so Monty pulls open two of them.

"Ok let's get these fuckas medicated and loaded up so we can get home to our families." Jax states dropping the dude on the table while I drop the broad in the wheelchair. I get the syringes ready and inject them both with the special serum Meech designed to basically put them in a coma. Once we get them settled in their drawer with the rest of them and their IV's. We also make our rounds to our businesses just doing the normal show face for a few hours then check on our homes.

"Yo did you read Meira's text yet?" I ask as soon as I hop in the backseat of the Monty's Range Rover.

"Yea she got buddies location but I'm not worried about that nigga right now the triplets are teething. It's time to get back home." Monty declares pulling off to head to the airstrip our jet is at.

"Besides it maybe time to let Meech and them handle shit more often. We have trained them to be the best of us. Nigga we have kids now and I don't know about you but I'm not trying to miss shit." Jax confesses next and I couldn't agree more.

"I feel the same damn way. Besides if they need their big brothers they know we always got them. Sounds like we are having an arakunrin ipade when we get back." They nod their response and hold up their fist for a bump that I gladly give.

"But what are we going to do about Marsh and Bree crazy asses?" Inquiring minds want to know because those to psycho's been wildin.

"Right now nothin. I haven't seen any news alerts lately maybe whatever the hell they had going on they got out of their system." He reveals as we board the jet. We get a text mid-flight that something has happened to baby Jackson, and they are going to the hospital.

"What the actual fuck is going on?" Jax says jumping in the driver's seat of one of our Tahoe's about to pull off without Monty and me.

"Damn nigga you were just going to leave us?" I question this nigga who is clearly on one now.

"Don't piss me off right now D. I'll throw yo ass out this fuckin truck." He threatens and as much as I know that fool loves me, I know his ass will and I'm not even mad about it so I just lean back in my seat and shut up. With the way this man sped through traffic I am shocked we didn't get pulled over before making it to the hospital. The moment he gets the truck fully in park him and Monty are out the truck then head straight for the emergency entrance with me right on their heels. The lady at the front desk recognizes us and sends us right to the room they have Jackson and Meira but the moment we get up there we hear shouting.

"Get the fuck away from my baby lady before you need one of these hospital rooms and I wish the hell you two would enter that room, I will have you badges for trophies." We hear Meira shout, and we all take off running towards her voice. We find her standing in front of a sliding glass door which we recognize to be the room baby Jackson is in.

"What the hell is going on here?" Monty questions as we walk up next to Meira then Jax goes to her other side, and I stand behind her.

"Sir who are you?" The white lady with bad fitted skirt suit and crooked glasses asks.

"I'm her husband and these are my brothers. Now answer my damn question." He demands as he rubs the back of Meira's neck to calm her down before she kills this lady in front of these cops.

"Well Mr. Fredericks the child is being taken into CPS custody due to suspicions of abuse, and your *wife* is being combative. So, you need to get her under control so we can do our job." This white bitch must have a damn death wish cause if Meira doesn't killer her one of us will. We equal opportunity life enders around here.

"She's right you aren't taken our child anywhere and I don't have to get shit under control. Ife mi what happened?" Monty declares with that air of confidence and power he always gives off in waves then turns to Meira to see what happened. I notice Jax to my left typing away on his phone and I already know who he's contacting which means we are trying the civil way first.

"MJ and Ayomi were with the Za'Meir and them and Jackson was with me in my workshop since he was having a "he only wants mommy day". I put him in his swing and turned it on and went to work but I didn't realize I sat the glass cup I was drinking out of close to the edge so when I bumped into the table getting up from my seat the glass fell and burst when it hit the floor sending glass everywhere. I thought it was just a few small cuts on his leg but then they wouldn't stop bleeding, so I rushed him here. The doctors started working on him and they couldn't figure out what was wrong, and his body isn't accepting the blood they are trying to give him, so he had an allergic reaction. He... he..." She falls into his arms crying and I turn to see our little man looking so helpless in the bed with a tube in his nose and IV running into his little arm.

"Check your phones and get the fuck away from my family before I get pissed off." Jax finally looks up from his phone with a stern, try me if you want to look on his face.

"I want that asshole of a doctor off my child's case as well the moment I walked in here he was talking down to me like I'm some fucking idiot. I kept telling him he must have a blood disorder since he won't stop bleeding then these fools showed up and I know they only did because I was alone." She expresses and I go searching for the nurses to point in me in the direction of said doctor. I found one of the nurses and immediately wished I didn't find nurse thirsty as Meira liked to call her. I knew they moved her but damn to the kids ward the fuck why. Luckily another nurse walks up before I have to speak to her.

"Hi I need the doctor on Jackson Fredericks case." I request as soon as I get close to her.

"And who are you sir?"

"His uncle and his mother right there is requesting him off his case immediately. Also make sure you request for your administrative director to come down as well." I inform her with the same air of authority my brothers carry letting her know not to question me. She moves behind the nurse's station and requests Doctor Pierce to come over then I head back to the fam. I note the CPS agent along with the security she had with her are now gone so, I enter Jackson's room and find Monty with Meira on one side and Jax on the other side kissing his little forehead then I go stand next to him.

"So did buddy ever give him anything for the reaction or get the bleeding to stop?" I can't help but rapid-fire questions after seeing him lying up in this bed with his chunky leg all wrapped up. Doctor Pierce comes strutting his ass in the room without knocking and fixes his posture the moment he realizes the three of our big asses are in the room. That was the moment I knew that puss ass cracka was going to the range or somebody he loves, let's see how bestie feels later.

"Mhmm Ms. Fredericks I was told you requested to have me taken off your son's case, may I ask why?" He stands close to the door he just walked in and the director walks in right behind him.

"It's Mrs. Fredericks and you're off *OUR* child's case because you were dismissive to my wife and had you listened to her our son wouldn't be laying here like this." Monty's voice is too damn calm and that tells me one thing unless Meira says otherwise, we will definitely be having some fun tonight.

"Director get a competent doctor in her or we can find another hospital to donate an entire wing to." Jax adds and I see the moment the color leaves ol boys face. So, it clearly was some misogyny and racist shit going on with him and that just boils my blood even further.

"Mr. and Mrs. Fredericks I have already called one of our specialists in the moment I saw little Jackson's chart and we both agreed he is showing symptoms of having a blood disorder called Hemophilia. He will run some test to confirm once he arrives until then we need you all to get tested to confirm who's blood he will be able to receive without any allergic reactions which we can start now." Director Jones informs us. I recognize some of the tension leaving my brothers and best friends' shoulders but not all of it. We all go one by one to get tested and so do the rest of the family once they show up, apparently Meira was so scared she didn't say anything to anyone in the house, she just rushed to the car and left. They come in and take the blood from Jackson needed to run the test and just left as she was walking in the new room; they moved Jackson to.

"Mr. and Mrs. Fredericks nice to meet you I'm doctor Shyne your pediatrician that specializes in blood diseases. I hate that it's under these circumstances, but I assure you I will do everything to help your son." She greets us. In the room there are almost all the adults except for both our moms and Uncle Tone, they stayed home with all the kids.

"So, first things first Mr. Jax Fredericks your blood was the only one that didn't cause an allergic reaction for little Jackson, and they are testing the blood right now to confirm my suspicions that he has Hemophilia. The nurse should be coming in at any moment to hang the blood we already have to replenish all that he has lost. It also shows that they did give him a very small dose Emicizumab to slow the bleeding, however once the test confirms we will do factory replacement therapy instead. The results should be back within the hour but the nurse checked his wounds, and the bleeding has slowed down. So we are out of the woods for the most part. I will check back in with you when the results come back." She explains everything and it's like the whole damn family was holding their breath because we all sighed at the same time.

"Wait doc so Jax being the only one to be able to donate does that mean he's the father?" Meira asks her almost sounding scared to get the answer.

"His blood type is the only one that matched Jackson, so yes Mrs. Fredericks." She replies and she leaves the room. Meira steps slightly away from Monty and looks up at him like she is bracing for something.

"Ife mi I'm not mad bring your ass back here I already knew." Monty reveals and we all look at him crazy.

"And you didn't tell me nigga." Jax stands up right and crosses his arms over his chest.

"What does it matter you are a dad to all three even if biologically only one of them is yours. You're right though I should've said something arakunrin, congratulations though." His attempt at an apology is welcomed by Jax with a handshake since we all know emotions aren't his strong suit.

Chapter Fifteen

Kelia Frederick

It's the day of the kids party and everything has been going great. Last weeks scare with baby Jackson snapped everybody into full on family mode even Chase and Kenya seem to be on better terms lately. Jax, Monty, and Dean took the boys to get haircuts, and we had the girl's hair done yesterday but they are out with their grandmothers getting their nails done. Ever since the incident when Money was shot, they have reinforced the guards when we leave alone again so moms has one driving and the other goes where they go. The rest of us are at the house setting up decorations and getting all the pool accessories blown up. The pool came out so beautifully. It has to be about twenty feet by twenty feet but it's not a normal rectangle or square it swerves on the sides, the front part has a sandy beach before you walk into the pool with a tanning bed and splash pad for the little ones. It has a volleyball net towards the back end, a bridge before that to go over to the other side of the grotto that has a waterfall, plants, and small fire pits placed throughout the grotto then a large one on the other side to roast marshmallows and for those cold Alabama nights. The pool even has a swim up bar on the right that has a mini fridge under the bar. Money and Tru are putting the finishing touches on the fully equipped outdoor kitchen over under the large, covered patio area since their new large tricked out grill. They also fully stocked the outdoor fridge with everything the kids could want to eat or drink along with some adult beverages in the doors. I just finished blowing up the balloons in the bag I have and when I turned to grab the other bag of balloons I noticed La'Meira coming out the sliding doors with baby Jackson in one arm and MJ in the other then one of the nannies has Ayomi. They place them inside the large playpen with Delia. I still can't believe the four of them are already sitting up and trying to scoot. Mama Fredericks says they are moving out the way for another baby but that can't be true cause Meira can't even have any more kids.

"Hi babe what else needs to be done?" She comes and hugs me from the back then I turn to give her a quick kiss.

"Nothing really. Money, Tru, Chase, Meech, and Marsh have gotten all the decorations hung up. They even got the grill started up. Chase and Meech just finished seasoning up the meats and the chef said all the sides should be done in a few. I'm just finishing up the balloons." We wanted to get things set up without her doing anything since our poor girl has been feeling down after what happened with baby Jackson. Our moms tried to get her to understand if that accident didn't happen with her, it would have happened another time and she may not have been there to make sure he got the care he needed. We hoped the video of the boys masked up with the arrogant doctor hang off his balcony upside down with his chest and stomach all red from the fellas smacking him on it would cheer her up. It gave her a small and light laugh for a moment but she crawled back in her shell the next day.

"Ok well moms should be back soon, but the boys are already on their way home. They stopped to grab the water guns they wanted and those gel blaster guns. These fools are about to have a field day back here. Did they gas up the atv's yet?" I nod yes and point to the ten atv's lined up to the left side of the house.

"Hi Sweetness, bestie." Dean greets us as they all come out the house with multiple large bags. Monty and Jax give Meira a kiss on the cheek, seeming to uplift her mood a bit then Za'Meir wraps his arms around her neck giving her a kiss all over her face and she breaks out into a fit of laughter trying to get away from him.

"Suga how has she been?" Jax questions me after sitting in the seat she abandoned.

"She seems a little lighter today than yesterday. She finally put Jackson down to play with the others." I nodded my head towards the playpen and they both walked over to check on the kids.

"Ma everything looks great." Darius comes up next to me and gives me a kiss on the cheek then runs off to change clothes with Za'Meir in the full bathroom on the other end of the patio that has a large shower, double sinks, and two toilets. The party starts going into full swing once the girls and some of the kids friends show up. Meira, Bree, and I go get changed into our bathing suits and I can't help but smack their asses before we head back downstairs.

"Alright babe get shit started and have us missing in action for our kids birthday party." She warns me while Bree side eyes me letting me know she's with the shits too. Before we can get carried away Meira notices Kenya and snatches her ass into one of the rooms and we join her locking the door behind us.

"Kenya get to talking and don't bullshit me I'm not in the mood." Meira demands.

"Meira it's nothing just family stuff." She says dismissively. She has clearly forgotten who the fuck Meira is coming at her with that lame ass reply.

"So, what that means we're not family now?" Meira gets in her ass kicking stance with her hands on her hips. Before Meira can dig into her though the door bust open with our men rushing in.

"Ah wateva the fuck this was about to be can wait. Wife bring your sexy ass on and get in the pool with me. Ooooh all that ass humph." Monty groans after picking Meira up and throwing her over his shoulder. Jax smacks her ass as they pass him and walks out behind them. Dean snatches my ass up next, and Marsh does the same to Bree causing all that ass of hers to jiggle so I smack it again since the guys are walking side by side.

We get outside and the fellas finally put us down on our feet then we are hit with shots from the kid's water guns so we all run to grab one from the pile on the long outside dining table. We are all running around laughing and shooting each other with water guns, some of the kids are jumping in the pool to run away. I notice Uncle Tone putting out the burgers and hotdogs on the dining table and the kids instantly drop their guns then rush over to the table to eat. Meira and I put the water guns down then make them all line up before they make a mess everywhere. They find themselves seats and calm down for a bit.

"Bro you are lucky as hell to have two rich dads." One of Za'Meir's friends compliments him and he just nods.

"But it isn't weird that their brothers who sleep together?" The other questions and Meira and I almost spit out the water we are drinking.

"Nigga my dads don't sleep together they are only with my mom and I know I am lucky. My pops are the best and it has nothing to do with their money. My dads and uncles built our homes plus we go fishing, play games together, and my mom has been the happiest she's ever been since they've been around, but I will admit the money is nice though." He confesses, inciting a wide smile to form on Meira's face and we feel the fellas walk close on us. They've been standing behind us for a minute.

"It's really like we have eight dads if I'm being honest cause I can literally run to any of them, and they got me. Not to mention our moms they are the best too." Darius adds in and I lean back on Deans chest then look up at him. He has the biggest proud daddy grin on his face and so does Monty and Jax.

"Man remember when that crazy white lady was trying to take you from the school, I thought your parents were going to burn down the whole darn school." One of the friends chuckled.

"Right if looks could kill the way both your moms were looking at her, she would have been dead as a chicken with its neck wrang at the slaughterhouse." The other adds in and they all break out into a fit of laughter and we just shake our heads at their foolishness. The fellas take advantage of us listening to the kids conversation by snatching Meira and I up. We head over to the mini cave they had built into the grotto far off in the back which I am now thinking was on purpose.

"What are you three up to now?" I question as Dean pins me up against Monty's front as he leans against the back wall of the cave and I notice Jax sitting on the makeshift bench with Meira straddling his lap.

"Whatever do you mean Suga?" Monty places his hand on my hip then grabs me by my chin then turns my head up towards him and gives me a peck on the lips. He turns my head back towards Dean who gives me a deep sensual kiss that makes my knees weak. That kiss remind me of the night we first hooked up. We were standing in his room and I had just told him I'd never done anything like this before so he revealed himself. I was stuck for a few seconds at how fine he was and the way he caressed my body with his eyes told me all I needed to know.

"We just wanted some alone time with our women. We've been sharing y'all with our lil crumb snatchers for the past few hours." He admits as I come back to this moment and I just shake my head at their needy asses but I love it. The water is above my chest when standing in the middle of the cave and all of a sudden, they start pushing us towards the middle, pretty much surrounding us. My back connects with Meira and we both look over our shoulder at each other and we both know it's about to be some foolishness. Dean is in front of me with Jax in front of Meira and Monty standing to our side facing the entrance of the cave as he looks over our heads.

"My Phoenix you have been over doing it ever since the accident with Jackson and I need you to hear me clearly it was an accident, one that saved his life. You are a damn phenomenal mother of six beautiful children and you are allowed to have a moment of doubt or weakness but remember who the fuck you are and don't wallow in it. Now give me a kiss with ya thick as a snicker sexy chocolate ass." Jax pours into to her with his hand around her neck. He leans down giving her a nasty wet kiss with his tongue damn near down her throat. Shit had me rubbing my thighs together. Monty notices and I feel his hand that's been resting on my hip slide over then into my bikini bottom. He rubs on my clit and I can't help but bite my lip to keep from moaning to loud.

"You, my Sweetness. I need you to get out of your head, don't think I haven't noticed how much more time you've needed in your prayer/meditation room. We've had these conversations about you talking to us about what you're feeling. If you don't want to go through with knocking these muthafuckas off baby we can handle it. We can find another path to healing for you if that way is too dark." Dean thinks I'm having second thoughts and a part of me is but that's not all.

"It's not that it's too dark for me. I'm just shocked at how much I am liking the other side of y'all world. I never really put forth much thought about killing someone. I mean it's crossed my mind mildly but I've been having some dark ones lately. So that's why I've been in my room more. Just trying to process my feelings." I confess and then I feel Monty begin to rub on my sensitive bud again. I hear moaning from behind me and guess Jax is doing the same to Meira.

"You two go give us those nuts." Dean requests with one hand arm around my neck the other tweaking my right nipple through my bikini top.

"Yesss." We both moan then lean our heads back on each other's shoulder. Within minutes were both cumming and panting from our release.

"That's our good girls now let's get back to the family the kids should be done stuffing their faces and ready for the atv rides then the big dinner should be done." Dean praises us after giving me a quick but heated kiss that promises to be so much more later. The party continues through the night and all the kids are passed out all over the main house from the game room, kid's bedrooms, and the other lounge area. We are doing our rounds to make sure everyone is ok and they have enough blankets.

"Now this is what I always wanted my home to be like." Meira expresses as we stand in the doorway of the game room looking over the boys and their friends from school sprawled across the sectional and the floor.

"Same Meira. Home filled with love, fun, and peace. Thanks guys." I agree with her and we lock hands with each other as we lean back on the fellas.

"You two would have done this with or without us." Dean praises.

"True I'm just glad it's with us." Monty declares kissing the top of Meira's head and stroking my side. We both smile up at them then we head off to go to bed because they have worn our asses out today.

Chapter Sixteen

Dean Fredericks

We gave the women what they requested and had family time for two weeks now we are all loaded on the jet to head to KC. The bomb dropped last week about the abortions and cheating on her sister's part. That video our plant sent us was hilarious. When the pastor saw the video of her and his son going then coming out the hotel together outside the city he went off and forgot he was in front of his congregation. Her parents were so distraught and having a fit trying to say it wasn't her then the son's wife slapped the piss out of him screaming she wants a divorce. Church services has been empty for the most part to the point they even had a guest pastor.

"Baby they are about to release what your parents did to the church." I inform her after checking my messages from our plant at the church. She simply nods her head. We decided to do it now since most of them cut themselves off from their family after they left the camp it won't seem odd that they are missing if anyone does think to look for them. Besides I doubt whatever my lovely wife has in mind to kill them that it will leave anything left for them to find. We all load up into our awaiting vehicles once we get off the jet. Monty and I head to his home with the girls while Chase, Meech, and the others head to Meech's lab to get things set up for my Sweetness. We stop over to Monty's and the moment we get inside her phone starts to ring from an unknown caller but Kelia answers anyway.

"Hello." She answers and then puts it on speaker phone.

"You bitch, I know you had something to do with my life going to shits lately. You better find a way to fix this shit or else." The voice we all recognize as her sister comes through loud and clear.

"I'm not fixin shit. What's done in the dark always comes to light so stop being a grimy bitch and you won't have these problems popping up." Kelia shouts back then ends the call and blocks the number. Another call comes ringing and she doesn't immediately answer but decides too anyway.

"What?"

"Kelia why would you do this to us. You have embarrassed us in front of the whole congregation. We can never go back there now." Her mother comes through the speaker attempting to plead with her.

"I did nothing of the sorts. I don't even know what y'all are yapping about." She plays confused and for a second, I don't get why but I realize she wants to hear them admit everything.

"You know good and well what we are talking about. You revealing that your sister's husband's affair then sending his damn mistress to the church or revealing your sisters' abortions and sleeping with the pastor's son. Oh no what about us sending you to the camp that was meant to help your ungrateful ass." Her dad comes shouting at the top of his lungs.

"First off stop screaming at me like I am a child and secondly it just sounds like all your family secrets are coming to light. I can't believe your perfect daughter actually committed multiple sins are you going to find a camp that will beat them out of her too." She questions them, her voice laced with sarcasm.

"Your sister will repent for her sins, and we will forgive as God see's fit. Something you need to do and move on." Her mother admits.

"Wow so just a few I'm sorry and that's all huh. Well, I forgave you long ago doesn't mean I have to allow you to continue to abuse me while the one who commits adultery, kills her babies, and continues to lie gets away Scott free. So, like I told you before leave. Me. The. Hell. Alone. I no longer have parents." She finishes reading them the riot act and ends the call blocking that number as well.

"You need a minute baby?" I walk up behind her rubbing up and down her arms to soothe her.

"No, I'm perfectly fine. That truly felt good." She confesses and leans her head back for a kiss. Monty and I head to make us some breakfast since we didn't get to eat before we left. A message I've been waiting for comes through text and I look up at a grinning Meira then nod my head.

"Hey Monty, ya wife just messaged us the location of that white dude we've been looking for."

"Ok bet let's deal with him after we send the ladies home tonight." He decides and I'm cool with that seeing as he tried to take our Meira and our damn mother. I want them both safely at our compound when we deal with him and whoever his boss maybe. We sit down and eat the light breakfast we cooked up. The moment Jax is putting the dishes in the dishwasher though Meech is calling our watches.

"What's arakunrin?" Jax answers his call, and we gather at the island to hear what's going on.

"Nothing just letting y'all know what Ke requested is all setup and ready for her." He replies.

"Ight bet we on our way to you now." He declares ending the call and we all head towards the garage after making sure everything is clean with the alarm back on. The ride there is silent but thick with anticipation. I tap my watch at the gate entrance to Meech's lab since I'm driving and the heavy titanium gate slowly slides open. I tap my watch again once we make to the four thousand square foot warehouse entrance and the door lifts for us to enter. I park next to our brothers trucks and we hop out but the ladies know to wait on us so I walk around the truck to open the door for Kelia while Monty holds Meira hand to help her out.

"Damn this place is huge." She expresses as she gets out looking around the open area of the warehouse then we start walking towards the back to heading to the left of the autopsy room he held the bodies in.

"Uh damn the size why the hell does Meech have it so cold in here?" Meira questions crossing her arms over her chest then rubbing them up and down. Jax takes off his jacket and places it on her shoulder then she pouts her lips for a kiss that he obliges. We walk behind the butcher curtains to find Meech and the rest standing in front of a large plexiglass container with two people tied to a chair sitting inside, then another one sitting in front of one of those deep tubs that athletes take an ice bath in that is filled with water, and the other three spread around next to their own death traps.

"Well boo I keep it cold in here for the purpose of germs plus it takes a lot longer for bodies to smell when they decompose in the cold." Meech answers her question as he turns to pick her up in a hug and she giggles then he does the same to Kelia.

"Is this up to you liking Ke?" He questions turning her towards all the contraptions.

"Yes, it's perfect Meechy." She jumps up on her tip toes doing her happy dance and I realize at that moment just how perfect for me she truly is. I thought Meira would be the only that participated in this side of our life which I was cool with but having my wife join in is warming me up something fierce. A thought to get something special for my baby just popped in my head and I admittedly started typing on my phone.

"Ok so who's going first Suga?" Monty questions standing next to her.

"Those two. They're the ones that did the stupid electric shock therapy on us." She points to the two that are in the plexiglass container we saw when we entered the room.

"Say less oh and I was able to find the eels you wanted. Those damn things almost zapped Chase earlier." He laughs then turns on the switch to something that causes water to start filling the container. My woman loves animals, and she told me she once thought about being a veterinarian but was laughed at by her parents. Within minutes it's filled to their chest are with water, then small fish and what looks like shrimp start to enter, and soon he releases what looks like a dozen electric eels.

"I made sure they haven't been fed for a couple weeks so they should be good and hungry. Don't worry that didn't harm them." Meech informs her.

"I know Meech. Oop there goes the first shock from a couple of them." She announces it, getting excited. The container has to be good eight or nine feet long and another four or five feet wide, so they have more than enough room to spread around. The two techs inside bodies spasm the moment the shocks hit them, and they seem to go limp. Meech hits the switch, and more water enters the container causing the electric eels to be scared sending out more voltage. The other fish in the tank are either dead or in shock, no pun intended from the zaps and are just slowly floating to the top. Some of the eels begin to eat them and one nips off a piece of one of the tech ears, probably though it was a fish. They start to fight each other as some go for the same fish or shrimp and zaps the entire container then we notice they both go completely limp.

"Yup they are dead. Now we can drop these two back to their homes to be discovered since it will look like heart attacks but it's up to you Ke." Meech states looking at his watch.

"That would be good just put her ass in the tub with a blow dryer, to be on the safe side." I'm so proud of my baby, she is really starting to think like us but still in her own way. We walk over to another container with another two in it that has this large box connected to it with these screeching and scratching noises coming from it.

"Now these to left me in that damn dark room for days with no food and I had to get a damn rabies plus tetanus shot after getting bit by a fucking rat. Let them go." She commands and Meech presses a button on the remote in his hand and a trap door lift between the box with the strange noises and the container they are sitting in. Within seconds the reason for the screeching noise is revealed to be more than a hundred large rats rush into it and they begin crawling, scratching, and biting everywhere.

"How do you like the feel of it you bastards?" Kelia walks up to the container smacking it with her open hand and just continues to shout curse word after curse word. I start to step towards her to comfort her, but Meira pulls me back and shakes her head. It's hard to see her screaming and crying but I quickly realize she's releasing the pain that she has been holding on to for all these years. We move on since we know it's going to take a bit for the rats to devour their asses, and she slaps the shit out of the dude in front of the large tub. By now the last two have realized they are going to die so the air is thick with anticipation, dread, fear, and joy but we all know who that is coming from. She has Chase and Marsh drops him in the tub then she pushes him down until his head is covered just holding him there. She does it repeatedly until he goes limp then leaves him under water and asks for Marsh gun which he hands over to her without hesitation. She simply aims and shoots her between the eyes like I taught her. We don't even realize but we have been here for hours, and my wife cried, screamed, and punched through her healing process.

"Ugghhh I'm hungry now can we go Fredericks now, well after we clean up." She requests as she looks over herself with the dried tear stains on her face, blood stains on her sleeves. and partially wet clothes. The ladies go wait in the car as we clean up and make arrangements for bodies to be taken where they need while putting the others in barrels filled with a superacid that should have them completely dissolved by tomorrow. Once we get all that done, we hop in our trucks and head to our separate homes, well of course we end up with Monty, Jax, and Meira but in our own rooms. We end up taking a much-needed nap after getting cleaned up then checking in with the kids. We all have dinner together then take the ladies to the airport since they decided to take a red eye due to us flying back later. They say just because we always have the money doesn't mean we need to always spend it on damn jet fuel. Marsh and Money took they two that were to be returned to their homes back while we got suited up to pay white boy whose real name is Stephan Fern a visit at his warehouse. Since he has a few guards, we grab a few weapons for fun. We lay most of them out then snatch his ass up to bring him back to Monty's wax museum. He decided to tenderize his ass a bit since he missed getting in the gym the past few days then we questioned him way into the morning hours. Monty decided to have Meech just give him the serum he uses and he starts singing like a canary after that. When we finally finish with him with him by the afternoon time so we make our normal rounds to our businesses and hop on the jet to head home by almost midnight. When I get in the door, I am bum rushed by my son who seems shaken up, so I look around for any disturbance then Kelia comes around the corner.

"He had a nightmare that something happened to you guys." She informs me as she leans her head against the doorframe looking exhausted.

"Aww man dad and your uncles are all good." I assure him while still holding him in my arms and rubbing his back. I mouth for her to go to bed and she stretches then yawns before walking over to give me a quick kiss and head upstairs.

"Hey baby boy you want to have Uncle Monty whip us up some food and have a late game night?" He nods his head still holding on to me tightly.

"Look at me baby boy. Daddy is ok and I won't be traveling as much going forward besides ya uncles always have my back so I'm good ok." I reassure him again then bring him back into a tight hug kissing the top of his head. I swear since turning thirteen he's grown at least six inches before the damn summer over with I'll probably be looking at him eye to eye. I make him go get his robe and put on a shirt then we head over to the main house. I smell food the moment we enter and my stomach growls making us both laugh but when we get in the kitchen it's Meira whipping up food.

"Dove what are you doing up? I told your bighead ass husband to whip up something."

"Well, he told me my baby had a nightmare so I'm cooking up his favorite honey chickens, fried hard, and there is some leftover mac and cheese and cabbage from dinner." She replies, turning to hug my boy the moment he runs to her for a hug. I just shake my head because these kids are spoiled rotten. It's one o' clock in the morning and she is here frying and saucing up his favorite wings.

"I will bring it all up in a few minutes Monty is already upstairs with the guys getting the game room started up." She turns back to the stove and I walk over to give her a kiss on the cheek while squeezing on her fat ass.

"Aight now start something sir."

"I'll finish once my boy is good, I promise." I whisper into her ear before walking off to the elevator that Darius is waiting for me in down the hall. The game room is probably the size of some people's two-bedroom apartments with its own full-size bathroom. It has one larger screen area made from four fifty-five-inch tv's then another three seventy-five-inch tv's on the other three walls. The walls are all black but each tv has led lights surrounding them and under each cabinet that has a different gaming system for each tv. The girls tv on the left of the room only has the newest XBOX and Nintendo switch system on them. We have a large sectional in the middle then about eight of those beanbag gaming seats everywhere else in different colors. By the time Darius and Za'Meir choose the game we're playing Meira is coming up with the maid's food cart full of food, drinks, and other snacks because she knows we are about to be up all morning and part of the afternoon. I send Meira a text message to make sure her ass is us because I was not playing earlier. I don't care that it's seven in the morning, the babies are with the nannies, and the chef is in the kitchen getting breakfast ready. Monty, Jax, and Meech are slumped over taking a nap while Chase, Marsh, Money and Tru are still taking turns playing Mortal Kombat or COD so I step through one of the hidden doors. I walk through the hall until ii make it to the door for our Sinful Sanctuary then enter to find Dove sitting on the edge of the bed with her legs spread open with her grey nighty still own. As weird as it maybe to some we all only have sex in here together as her bed is strictly for her and Monty and the same goes for Jax's bed. No words or foreplay is needed right now so I strip out my clothes as I walk to her and she does the same. The moment I get close our lips lock with each other and our hands roam over each other's body. I slide balls deep on the first stroke and fuck at the edge of the bed until she is squirting and creaming all over the place.

Chapter Seventeen

Kelia Fredericks

It's been a couple weeks since I released all that had been a burden on my shoulders, and I swear I have never felt lighter in my life. My parents and even some people from the congregation have been blowing up my phone but between all the kids' football, cheerleading, gymnastics, karate, and dance practices plus getting them ready for school starting in a couple weeks I have been too busy to give a shit. Whoever said being rich makes life easier was a muthafuckin lie. It may make the cost of things easier to deal with but when you are an involved parent nigga that shit doesn't make much difference on all the damn running around, PTA meetings, sleepless nights baking shit for fundraisers, being the parent they always look at to pay for shit since they know you have money. I have even started allowing the guards to drive more often with all the running around we have to do most days with the fellas at work during the day or if they are here building one of our homes. I disappear sometimes to go sit in the acre size garden me and the ladies have grown over the many months across from the mini farm we have. Today though I am out with the girls and we just finished getting our nails and lashes done. Before we can all hop back into the truck that Murch is holding the door open to some man tries to walk up on us.

"Nah buddy back up. Who are you and what do you want?" Murch addresses him with his hand pushed out towards his chest, stopping him from walking any closer.

"You might want to move your hand unless you want to be arrested for assaulting a police officer." The man replies revealing his badge on his waist.

"First off, I know my rights as a licensed bodyguard, second, I am not touching you, third you walked up without identifying yourself and that was recorded on camera. Now name and badge number, officer." He educates the man who now looks pissed instead of the cool demeanor he had walking up on us. He runs his credentials by Murch who is quietly relaying them to the men on his watch.

"Ok you check out officer. How can I help you?" He questions him, finally putting his arm down.

"It's detective Patrick Crews and I have a few questions for Mrs. Fredericks about a missing person." He announces and he has all our attention.

"Any questions you have can be directed to her lawyer at this number. Ladies." Murch gives him Brinx's card then turns to gesture for us to hop in the truck and we do. Before we can drive off the guys are calling on Murch's watch, and he puts it on speaker.

"Yes sir's" He answers.

"What the hell did he want?" Monty's voice comes booming through the speaker like a roaring lion.

"He wanted to question Mrs. Fredericks about a missing person so I gave him Brinx's card and ushered the ladies into the truck." Murch explains sitting in the front seat looking around as he usually does and you can always tell this man is former military.

"I can always count on you Murch. Y'all headed home?" Jax comes through on the call next.

"Yes, *Big Papa* we have peopled enough for the day." Meira answers and we all agree. The ride home was silent with Bree tapping on her phone to Marsh of course, while Meira is texting Monty and Jax in their couples group chat, and Dean is blowing up my phone with back-to-back text. As per usual Kenya is playing Casper the friendly ghost but even further because she's out of town. I'm not sure what the hell is going on with her, but I don't think Chase is going to put up with it much longer and lawd let's not get to Meira, she already cornered her once. When we get to the house the men are all outside waiting on us looking like soldiers ready to go to war. Monty opens my door first since I'm on the end with Meira in the middle and Bree on the other end. He holds each of our hand to get out the car like we are royalty and that's what I've felt since being added to this family of crazy ass men. I walk over to my man who grabs me up in his arms like I've been gone for days or in some type of danger.

"Babe we're ok, relax." I assure him then give him a kiss on the lips and grab his face to lean our foreheads together so he can calm down.

"We watched the video, and he looks familiar, but I can't get quite put my finger on it." Jax informs us.

"True but he called the lawyer to set up an interview with Meira. He wants to question her about the coach going missing because he heard about what he tried to do with Za'Meir." Monty fills us in as we walk into the main house wrapped up in our men's arms. We head into the family room off the patio to continue talking and watch the kids have a ball in the pool, something they've been doing every day since it was finished.

"Look it's nothing to worry about just go in, answer the questions and come back home. They have absolutely nothing on you or any of us for that matter." Dean states from next to me on the loveseat.

"As much as I don't want you to even grace the doorstep of a police station with your presence Ife mi, he's right. Hell, there isn't even a body for them to connect to anything so even less to worry about."

"I made sure of that my damn self. I will gladly be your guard that day Meira." Money states. He has become very protective of Meira since becoming a part of the family. Well, he's protective of us all but something more for her.

"That's cool you and Murch, Money. I have a damn meeting I can't reschedule and Jax has the boys football stuff and Dean aren't you with the Za'Mara and Mercy at the karate tournament?" Monty runs down their schedules and decides it's best for both to go.

"Yea and Kelia will be with the Denise at gymnastics and Chase is going to have to take Mariah and Myla to dance." Dean adds to the schedule since Meira will need to be there. I know they aren't nervous about anything but I am. I don't need anything to happen to any of them, especially Meira, she's like the super glue to this family. Everyone plays their part but she's the spiritual one, the one that's always there for everybody, and man we all can cook but it's something about when she gets into the kitchen. That woman just spreads love with her presences.

"Ok that's enough of that mess. Alexa play my ninety's soul and R&B playlist." She commands and gets up to light her summer scented candles and the room becomes enveloped in the sweet aroma of sugar and watermelon plus a warm scent I can't quite put my finger on. She heads into the kitchen and starts gliding through with so much ease, seasoning the meat, chopping the veggies, and cleaning the rice before pouring it in a pot.

"Wait is she about to make her oxtails, cabbage, white rice, mac and cheese, and cornbread?" Meech asks when he comes in the house from playing with the kids a bit.

"Yup." Monty answers rubbing his stomach that's still pure abs even with the way he puts away food, hell how all of them eat for that matter.

"Well, I'll be comatose tonight. That meal is every fucking thing." Meech says dropping in the armchair closes to him.

"That's love nigga." Jax expresses getting up from his seat to walk over to Meira in the kitchen then proceeds to grab her in his arms to dance with him to Jill Scotts "The Way" while everything simmers. Monty grabs him a drink from the bar nearby and sits back in his chair and just watches them with a smile on his face. When I first saw those three together, I was sure some jealousy was bound to happen, but they just mesh so damn well, and each understands their rolls within their dynamic. Even with the five of us it's like strawberries and chocolate separate tasty but together it's a delicate party of flavors in your mouth that compliment each other. Before I can protest Dean grabs my hand to pull me from the couch to sway to one of my favorite songs by the beautiful Aaliyah.

"Oh, lawd they having grown folks time." Za'Meir says walking through the sliding glass door with the others.

"Awwww mommy and Papi are dancing." Za'Mara coos as she walks in behind him.

"Welp looks like we're going to grandma's house tonight. Let's slide y'all." Denise says and we all laugh when they all about face out the sliding glass doors to walk over to the grandparents' house. It's kinda sad to think my parents could have been apart of all this but they chose to be hateful instead. Once our dance session is over the fellas set the dinner table while we get the food put in the serving bowls and start placing the bowls on the table. Meira sits at the head of the table with Monty to her left and Jax to her right, Dean next to Jax with me next to him, then Chase and Kenya across from us, Marsh and Bree next us, Money, Meech, and Tru are at the end of the table.

"Damn this shit is good per usual, Meira." Chase expresses sucking the meat off the bone but the way he is making that damn slurpy noise and that tongue ring is gleaming under the light is doing something to my pussy right now. I look over to Meira then Bree and they are clearly having the same thoughts I am having.

"Chase, you keep sucking and slurping on those oxtails like that I'm going to give you something to really slurp on." Meira warns him but the look on his face says he was waiting for that.

"Don't threaten me with a good time Meira. I've been waiting for these three to let me at you." He throws back at her as he looks right at her wrapping his tongue around another piece of oxtail pulling it into his mouth then pulling it out with two of his fingers and the bone is naked. No gravy, meat, nothing. Dammit I think I identify as an oxtail now. Meira looks at Monty then at Jax who both nod their approval. The room becomes thick with anticipation of what Meira's ass is going to do. When we finish dinner no one moves immediately but Meira does after a few seconds and struts her way over to Chase's side of the table. When Chase slides his seat back, she pushes the dishes to the middle of the table then hops that juicy ass of hers on the table, places her feet in his lap then spreads her legs to sit her feet on either arm of the chair. Chase scoots his chair closer then grabs her by her thick chocolate thighs putting her ass on the edge and pushes her to lean back on her elbows. Her dress rolls up to her waist and we all sit back watching as sucks and slurps on her pussy even sexier then when he was eating the food. Meira is clearly enjoying because her head is leaned back, eyes rolling to the back of her head, and she is grinding her hips against his face. He's so invested in eating her pussy he gets out the chair and drops to his knees then starts flicking that damn tongue ring against her clit.

"Chase... Chasssee... Fuck I'm cumming." She moans with her voice hoarse from screaming every obscenity that comes to mind with the way he has her pussy dripping. Before I can make my way over there, she starts squirting but he latches on to her clit and I see the moment she starts creaming all down his beard. I drop next to him and start licking up every drop from his beard then when he turns towards me letting up on her I lick it off his lips. He pulls me in for a kiss then sucks her juices off my tongue and I can't help but moan feeling like electricity is lightly running through my body straight to my damn pussy. I just know my shit dripping on the floor since I decided to forgo panties tonight in hopes of some freaky shit happening. He grabs me by my neck continuing to kiss me for a few seconds then turns me towards her pussy and I finish licking up the juices that leaked out.

"Mhmm fuck Ke babe." She whispers as I swirl my tongue around her clit sucking it between my lips and flicking my tongue over her sensitive bud until she's rubbing her pussy on my face this time. I feel Chase come up close next to me and sticks his tongue in her pussy. I let go her clit to lick my way down to slide my tongue in next to his and I feel her pussy clench around us.

"Fuck now that's some sexy shit." A soft voice I recognize as Bree's groans then when I look up from Meira's pussy the table is cleared, and she is on her hands and knees next to Meira palming one her breast through her dress before pulling it down. She grabs one of her breast then flicks her tongue over her nipple then sucks it into her mouth.

"Fuck... fuccckkk." Meira screams out bucking and twisting her hips against our face. We lick up the juices that are leaking out her pussy then we both slide our tongues out and back up to her clit gliding our tongues side to side. When Chase slides two of his long thick fingers into her pussy I add two of my own stretching her shit out. We stroke her shit in sync and the noises her pussy is making causes me to take my other to rub on my clit.

"Oooooh fuck." She moans then her legs start to shake which signals she is about to have the most euphoric orgasm and boy was I right.

"Damn Meira your pussy taste sooo fucking good." Chase growls against her clit and before we know it she is squirting, and so much creamy goodness is all over our fingers you can barely see our skin tones. We keep stroking her pussy through her orgasm. Once her shaking subsides completely we slowly slide our fingers out her pussy and she twitches.

"That felt fucking amazing." She groans, still slightly out of breath. I lean back on my calves with my knees spread as I'm still rubbing on my clit.

"I see you rubbing on that fat pussy Suga." Jax groans as he leans over to grab me off the floor then places me on the table next to Meira who now has Bree naked and riding her face while she leans forward sucking Monty's fat chocolate dick, drool sliding down both sides of her mouth. Jax starts rubbing his flat tongue side to side across my clit I can't help but to buck my hips forward and tighten my thick thighs around his neck. Chase is now balls deep in Meira's pussy working his hips in a circular motion and when he pulls it out it looks like its covered in vanilla ice cream. I look to my left and notice Meech has his fat dick buried deep down Kenya's throat as he sits in his seat with his head leaned back, she decided to show her shady ass up about an hour before dinner was done. I travel my eyes lower when I notice her hips moving to see she's riding Money's face. Dean turns my head towards him as he stands next to me at the head of the table.

"You enjoying yourself Sweetness?" He inquires with his deep groggy voice that's heavy with so much lust like the air in the room.

"Ooooh fuck yes daddy." I moan due to Jax sliding his large, long fingers in my pussy while simultaneously slurping on my pussy. I hear so many grunts and fucks around me as Dean turns my head towards the edge the table and taps my chin with his dick.

"Open up. Mhmm just like that." He growls low as he pushes his dick to the back of my warm inviting throat. I feel him tap on that the thing that hangs in the back of my throat, and I hum. Another orgasm hits and comes on so hard I almost black out as Dean is still feeding me his dick. The feel of Jax massive dick sliding into my wet walls causes my orgasm to continue to wash over me. We must go at it for another thirty minutes before I see Monty snatches Meira up once Marsh grabs Bree once Monty cums. They all head upstairs while Dean and I head home fully satisfied.

Chapter Eighteen

Dean Fredericks

So, we are all getting ready to go our separate ways but no one wants to leave as Meira is getting ready to head to the police station.

"Brinx, Money, Murch I am trusting y'all with my soul. Bring her back." Monty jabs his finger towards the ground to convey his point. They all nod their heads and load up into the SUV to head there.

"Monty she's going to be fine remember your words they have absolutely nothing they can arrest her for." I try to assure my big brother because I can see the pain in his eyes as the truck drives away.

"I know but something in my gut is not sitting right with me, but I can't put my damn finger on it." He replies and I know what he means. I just started running our facial recognition software on that detective Crews because I know we know that paper thin white boy from somewhere. I load the girls up into my SUV next with Jax right behind us in his and everyone else back-to-back. Once we make it to the main road, we all go in different directions.

"That's my babygirl, lay him out." I cheer for Za'Mara when she slams the little boy she's up against and I give the other parents who look at me the universal black face for what nigga. Mercy went first with her belt class and it's almost over, but they decided they wanted to ride with Za'Mara's bestfriend. I called Tru to be their guard while they're out and about with their friends since he's her favorite plus I need to get back to see what's going on with Meira. By the time they are announcing my babygirl as the winner just like Mercy was my phone is ringing with a call from Jax. I snap a few quick pictures then walk outside the gymnasium to answer.

"Arakunrin."

"Mannnn these lil muthafucka's just tried to jump Za'Meir and I only say tried because his friend and Darius jumped in. His own fuckin teammates bru." Jax voices come roaring through the phone so loud I have to pull that bitch from my ears and I still hear him loud and clear.

"Wait, what?" I question the moment it registers what the hell he just told me.

"You heard me they tried to jump him because they were mad, some how it's already gotten around town that Meira was taken in for questioning on the coaches missing case. One of those bastards hit my boy with a damn helmet in the shoulder he was shot in cause he was getting his ass beat. When I made it over there the boys were slinging, their ass left and right. Brex ass is family now, he was hopping on their asses about Za'Meir." I hear the anger in his voice, and I already know we aren't physically touching anyone, but somebody's life is about to be fucked up.

"Say less I will have Kelia get into with his mom. I know his pops not around much but he's good now." I send a text to Ke as well as Bree because I know he has a little sister too and they will get them right.

"Facts but I'm headed to the urgent care since my baby is still at the police station for some odd fuckin reason to make sure Za'Meirs shoulder is ok." I hear the worry in his voice as we end the call and now that I think about it has been a while since they made it there. I go back in to give the girls a kiss as Tru is walking in.

"Hi, Uncle Tru, you with us today?" Za'Mara asks as she looks up to him and he nods his head yes causing her to do her happy dance. Tru and I look at each other with a smile and shake our heads at her silliness.

"No word on Meira yet?" He inquires as I am about to dap him up to leave and I shake my head then leave to go home. I make a stop to my office first to pull up the facial recognition software and end up falling down a rabbit hole once the computer shows his other identities. My watch starts going off with messages from my brothers and I realize I've been sitting her for hours, so I just shut down my computer then head home.

"What's with all the damn messages." I question the moment I walk into the main house.

"You'd know if you checked your messages that they kept Meira." Monty shouts when he stands from his seat in his office.

"I told him it was nothing I could do they are well within the law to hold a potential suspect for at least seventy-two hours." Brinx defends himself standing from his seat then says he will be in contact with us if anything changes. Money gives me a look to not say anything, so I ball my fist up and place it behind my back for my brothers to see before they all start going off on Brinx. The moment the cameras on the tv on the far wall shows he's getting in his car, Monty remotely locks every door and Jax sends a text in the family group chat for everyone to stay put.

"What's going on?" He questions.

"Money?" I turn to him to see what's up.

"Something up with that nigga. Meira turned on her mic when they were in interrogation for Murch and I to hear and that nigga was letting them rag on her way to much for my liking. Called her a glorified escort that lucked up and married a rich thug who protects criminals. That nigga didn't say shit until they said they thought she was covering for you and to just tell the truth." Money explains.

"What the fuck and you let him leave Money?" Jax questions him standing from his desk on the other side of the room.

"There's more isn't there Money?" Monty asks him next.

"Meira when she was in there, she said a Calder's name like there was a connection between him and the detective. Then when they were moving her to holding, I almost lost my shit, but she told me to get home and tell y'all but Calder is dead how could he even send anyone after her." He finishes explaining then falls back into his seat with a heavy sigh.

"I don't think it's Calder but the same person who sent old boy after moms in KC. He's just using Calder's people. The facial recognition pulled these for detective Crew. He was on Calder's payroll back in KC to hide his sex trafficking amongst other discretions. I found payments from one of Calder's old Cayman Island accounts going back at least six years. I tried tracking the payments he received from the new person, but they are a lot smarter than Calder was."

"I found something out about the coach and Kelia's parents as we all aren't about to like." Monty looks at all of us and he has our full attention now.

"They both had offshore accounts setup days before starting shit with the family and then a hundred k was deposited into each of them once they made contact or attempt was made. I couldn't track that fuckin account either." He finishes and my blood boils so hot I swear you can see steam blowing out of them.

"Wait were you able to get the last four at least and were they 8596?" I ask to see if it's the same account I found.

"So, it's one person trying to fuck with our family." He says letting me know it's the same.

"I thought that him coming for Meira after so long and knowing who she's married to was weird. The police officers will soon learn that their prized coach had a habit of blackmailing the single mothers of his football players into sleeping with him but all of them were single. Then he also waited for a while which wasn't his MO." Jax adds in and has all of us looking like what the fuck.

"Ok what loose ends if any have, we left behind that actually have the resources available to plant a dirty cop in our district, pay over one hundred k to Kelia's parents as well as her sister, Coach, and hire a mercenary to kidnap our mom by paying off her sorry as boyfriend." Monty questions us all. I must take a seat and think about that shit because doing what they did on the level they have done takes a lot of resources.

"Wait if the detective is dirty don't we need to get Meira the fuck out of that place even faster. It's no telling what he's actually holding her for and it's a lot that can happen in seventy-two hours." Money questions.

"I already texted Brinx to get his ass on it and sent him the women I found that he blackmailed plus we have a few officers and detectives on payroll that are looking out for her. They will also be dealing with our crooked detective for us." Jax assures him.

"So, the only ones I think could have done this, but I'm not convinced are Artemis parents but that's only if they found out it was us that got rid of him, maybe Justin's dad but he wrote him off a long time ago, or maybe somebody who worked with Calder." Monty contemplates out loud.

"Ok we are going to divide and concur like we usually do but don't poke the hornets' nest this is just information gathering. We don't need anyone not looking for us to start looking." Jax directs everyone being his normal calm and collective self when Monty isn't thinking straight. We sit there for the next few hours trying to track down who the hell could be after the family. Monty, Jax and I have to occasionally leave to check on the kids then right back to it. We work well into the morning, and the kids decided they didn't want to do anything until their mom and auntie comes home. We are back to trying to track down the money when we hear the front door opening and we know none of the kids are going out the door since we made them breakfast, they went straight to the game room. The eight of us come into the living room as the ladies come downstairs at the same time and rush Meira the moment, we realize it's her.

"Unhand my wife." Monty shouts walking over to the ladies who have surrounded her at the door.

"Ife mi." He calls to her and she runs to jump in his arms. Jax walks up next to them, and she wraps one of her arms around his neck to pull him closer then gave him a quick kiss.

"I just need a good bath. I'm ok y'all I promise." She wiggles her body so Monty will put her down.

"I'll run ya bath babe come on." Kelia instructs her as she grabs her arm, and they head upstairs.

"Brinx office." Monty demands with his jaw clenched and I know Jax is too quiet for my liking. Sure enough, the moment we get into the office Jax has Brinx has him jacked up on the wall with his hand around his throat, squeezing tight.

"I don't know what the fuck your problem is with my woman but you better fix that shit really fast before I skin your ass alive and feed you to my wolves Brinx." Jax threatens then drops him on the floor.

"Look I'm sorry I let my jealousy get the best of me." Brinx confesses.

"Jealous for what nigga?" Monty yells from behind his desk.

"It's just we been brothers in arms for years and you welcome this young nigga out of nowhere to come live with your family. I felt some type of way." He further confesses and I swear I want to knock his head between their desks.

"Nigga my wife runs this shit, and I'm not shamed to admit it. She's an empath so she probably sensed that shit in you and that's why she's not that fond of you. Now all you did was piss ha off."

"The women run this compound, and they all look up to her besides our mothers she goes to them for comfort. You better be lucky she didn't kill you on the way here and I'm sure she only didn't off the strength of Monty." I add in trying my hardest to restrain myself.

"I know I know. That's why the moment I had time to sit with it, and you sent me the evidence on the coach I went straight to the police station. I sat there all night until a judge was available that would make them release her." He admits finally getting off the floor.

"That's cool and all nigga but I'm not sure we can trust you anymore." I tell him but before he can defend himself Meira comes in swaying her sexy ass wide hips wearing one of her silk moo moos and behind her are our ladies including both our mothers. She stops kissing each of us on the cheek before heading over to Monty and Jax, who are now standing on either side of her.

"You guys didn't tell me he was abandoned as a child and grew up in foster care." She announces and that partially makes his actions understandable but only partial. She comes from around the desk gesturing with one hand for him to come to her with her other hand in her pocket. When he gets close, she pulls him in with a one-armed hug and before we can register the simple gesture, she has a taser jammed into his side.

"You feel that? It's about fifty thousand volts of electricity going through your body. I am going to need you to remember this pain any time that jealousy bone of yours acts up because you cross my family again it will be ten times that coursing through your body until all that is left of you are ashes, understand?" He's fallen to his knees, his body jerking from the continued voltage, and is in so much pain all he can do is nod.

"Good boy. Now I'll be with my babies in the playroom and before any of you ask, I've already eaten these two made me eat while I was in the tub." She says then sashays right back out the room.

"Now that is dealt with. I feel like we haven't made much headway with finding out who the piece of shit that set all this mess in motion in the first fuckin place." Monty slams his fist on his desk visibly frustrated. We fill Brinx in on what we have found out thus far and we get back to trying to figure things out.

Chapter Nineteen

Kelia Fredericks

It's been a few days since Meira came home, and I swear I'm sick of people coming for our family. We had a family meeting the other day about all the shit that's been going on and they told us about the payments made to my parents as well as the coach. They were having a hard time trying to figure out who sent the payments. They made some headway yesterday though; Monty was able to get one of his connections to give him the name of the shell company on the account. The detective has been trying to get each of us to come in for an interview, but Brinx has been shutting down every attempt. He did call in at least three of the mothers on the list they handed in to bring Meira home and it's about six more. That saggy balls shrimp dick Dr. Egg head ass nigga has been harassing women for years. Jax and Meech just left for something that came up at their club and restaurant. I'm in the back in La'Meira's workshop packing orders because she needed to help Monty run through all these shell companies that were connected to the one that made the payments. I find me a groove with my music then someone decides to call me, and I see on my watch it's not the fam but an unknown number. I haven't heard from my old family in a bit so unfortunately it can possibly be one of them and sure enough it's my mother as I recognize her voice the moment it comes through on my speaker crying.

"What do you want now?" I sigh as I am not in the mood for her theatrics.

"They... they killed your sisterrrr." She comes bawling and shouting. I simply roll my eyes not moved at all by her revelation.

"Ok what did she do for them to kill her?" I ask only mildly interested seeing as I know these dummies accepted money from someone pretty bad.

"What did she do? Really Kelia, we didn't raise you to be hateful." She attempts to chastise me but I'm barely paying her any attention. I sent a text to Dean to let him know what happened.

"Mrs. Black I already know you took money from some very bad people so whatever is happening to your family sounds like you're getting your just desert. So, what exactly can I help you with?" I ask her to try to get to the point of her phone call because I just know this woman does not think I give a shit after everything they've done to me.

"Look I know we didn't raise you the way you feel like we should have but we are still your family, and we know you have the money to protect us. This is all your faults after all, if they weren't after you, we would've never been in the cross hairs." I can't believe she just justified taking money from someone to try and take my child from or whatever else their plan was on us. I can't help but laugh because this is next level delusional. I try to stop laughing long enough but it takes me a minute or two.

"Are you done? This is a serious situation they hung your sister from her bedroom window for Christ sakes. What type of people are after those thugs you call men?"

"I am done. Can't help ya and good luck." I end the call and before I can call my husband he is walking through the workshop doors with lunch. I walk over to the empty table where he sits the food containers down on then pulls out a stool for me to sit on. He lets me take a few bits of my food before he starts in with the questions and all I can do is giggle.

"Sooo what did she want besides saying someone killed your sister." He questions.

"She asked for us to protect them after insulting y'all by calling y'all thugs. Oh, and blamed us for them taking the money they offered her to try to take our baby from us to give to my grandma dress wearing lopsided titty ass sister." I inform him of the foolishness said then get quiet for a bit to finish eating my steak and chicken hibachi.

"What do you think about helping them maybe putting them up in a hotel or something?" I like at my husband like he's grown two fucking heads because he clearly must have or something else is going on with him.

"You're joking right?"

"No, I don't want you to think that you have to be like us. Let's face it my brothers and I are not poster kids for the emotion norm." He explains and I lean over the table to give him a brief kiss.

"I don't know if it's anger and or hurt still telling me to say no or if it's my clear-headed side saying no." I confess because I really don't know.

"Well how about this I text the fam and we can have a quick family meeting to see what everyone else thinks. Maybe that will help you make sure you're thinking clear-headed." He offers a solution, and I nod yes because hearing their perspective may just help me figure out my feelings since I can't seem to myself. We continue to eat, and he even helps me pack up some more orders to have the post office pick up in about an hour. We hop on the golf cart and head to the front gate with the bag full of orders to hand them off to the guard. Once we make it back to the house everyone is in the family room waiting for us.

"Ok y'all my egg carrier called asking for us to help since it's our fault she is in trouble after taking the money from said person who has now killed my sister by hanging her outside her bedroom window." I sit and get straight to the point but of course none of this faze them. They just sit and wait for me to make my decision.

"So, we called everyone to ask y'all opinion on whether or not we should help them since I can't seem to figure out how I feel about it. Dean suggested maybe we just put them up somewhere in a hotel for a bit, since y'all are tracking down that person anyways." I finish then sit back in my chair.

"Well babe you know I'd say plant some cameras in their home to see who comes after their asses but at the end of the day you operate with more of a conscience than we do. So, for your sake I would say help them hell put them in one of the trailers near the guard's post." Meira suggests something that makes me think for a moment. Could I really leave my parents to die when I could've helped them or my brother, but he moved years ago hopefully they won't even go after him. He wasn't as bad as our sister, he just never said anything or stood up for me, so I guess in a sense it actually makes him worse.

"Why put the guards out, just put them in my house and I'll continue to stay here. Not like it's much of a home anyways." Chase offers his place for them to stay and throughs a jab at a silent Kenya. She folds her arms over her chest and sighs heavily with an eye roll.

"Sounds fine to me. I want to keep an eye on their asses anyways cause I feel like they are up to something." Meira agrees and makes an observation that hadn't crossed my mind but now is running rampant. They all look at me for a final decision. I love the amount of support and love they give me that I missed growing up.

"You know Meira is right I don't think I could feel right leaving them out there to get killed even though I hate their asses plus we may need to be watching them." I decided and they all nod their heads in agreement. Bree and Meira say they are going to check to make sure Chase has filled the house with the basics. I make the call to my donors.

"Look we will help you this time but once the danger is clear y'all can gone on about your lives. Jax and Meech will be there to get you in an hour pack only what you need and y'all will be staying in my brother-in-law's home once y'all arrive. Oh, and don't think y'all are getting anywhere near my children." I give them the run down and don't give them time to protest since I hang up on them the moment I finish my sentence. Dean and I have a talk with the kids to let them know about my donor's arrival but to form their own opinions about them, but Delia is to not be anywhere near them ever. The kids go on there way to ride the atv's with their cousins. The time flies by waiting on my donors to arrive with Jax. We received the text a few hours ago from Jax that they had them and made sure they weren't followed to their private hangar before taking off. Now they are coming down our long u-shaped driveway and I am now second guessing my decision to bring them here to interrupt my peace. We wait for them on front of Chase's and all the men decided to make their presence known.

"The moment they start making you feel uncomfortable their asses are being shipped out to the next motel." Monty assures me stroking my shoulder from behind me while Dean stands to my right and Meira to my left, both holding my hand. Jax hops out first and if looks could kill whoever was pissing him off would be dead.

"Kelia yo parents almost didn't make it here. I truly never met a woman I wanted to put my hands on as much as your mother." He sighs deeply, picking up Meira for a hug and to calm his nerves. I look up at Dean and he just winks at me trying to get me to smile, which he succeeds in doing so.

"Sheesh all this money and y'all could spring for a separate truck for us to ride in with our luggage instead of with this behemoth of a man." My egg carrier complains the moment she gets out the truck and I snap.

"Now wait a damn minute what you are not going to do is disrespect my family and the help they are giving you off the strength of y'all being the people that created me. What you will do is take y'all ungrateful behinds in this house and stay there until we tell y'all the coast is clear. No roaming around our property without a guard, you prepare your own meals and clean behind yourselves, do you understand?" I walk up on them pointing my finger at her chest with a look of disgust on my face.

"Little girl I don't kno-"She starts to say but I cut her off.

"You heard what I said and it's not up for negotiations. If you cause any disruption in our peace both of your asses are gone. Don't test me. See I'm starting to regret it already." I say turning back to my husband and the rest of our family. We put Tru on them since we needed to make sure the guard couldn't be sweet talked by an old couple then left to go back to the main house.

"I let them keep their old phones, but I cloned them when they weren't looking so whatever messages they get we get." Jax announces once we all sit down in the family room to watch the kids play in the back while the babies are on the floor crawling around in their play pen. It's been four days since they've been here and under Tru's watch, they have been behaving more than I expected them to. The only hiccup we had was them trying to come over to see Delia and my father thought it was a good idea to try to swing at Tru when he told him no. Seeing Tru put my sperm donor on the ground like that healed something else in my spirit.

"Ahhh shit we may have a problem." Dean says, popping his head into the kitchen from his office.

"What's wrong baby?" I question him as I walk into office with his breakfast since the kids wanted to sleep in today and baby girl already got her titty she back down for a nap.

"A text just came through on your parents' phone about did they get what they wanted yet because they're coming." He informs me of what just came through on their phone and I knew Meira was right about them being up to something. Clearly, they wanted Delia whether they were offered that money or not.

"I just messaged my brothers to prepare the guards for someone possibly trying to get on the compound. Extra guards are already on the way. Wait there's another text coming through. They want to know what they know about the layout of our property. I'm glad you told them no wondering the property unsupervised." He continues.

"I knew I shouldn't have brung their asses here. It was all a setup." I shout out my frustration. He says my parent's text back they need more time but whoever they're texting tells them they have two hours to get what they want and get out.

"Hey some of the guys from KC are on their way on the company jet. How much time do we have?" Monty informs us as he and the others all walk into Deans office one by one kissing my cheek as they come.

"We only have two hours. The KC team can be back just in case we actually need it. The twenty guys from the firm here with the fifteen we already have roaming the property will have to be enough." Dean brings everyone up to speed on the text as they continue to come in and I get angrier by the second.

"I'm putting a bullet in their heads NOW!" I shout grabbing one of the guns out his secret compartment by the door and rush out the house to Chase's with everyone on my heels but something has taken over me. I make it to the house quickly gaining access using my watch and rush upstairs where I hear their voices in one of the bedrooms. I kick in the door and fire a shot at the wall purposely missing their heads.

"You worthless, ignorant, sack of shits. You only came here to try and steal my damn child AGAIN!" This shot goes through my father's shoulder since they are cowering in the far corner of the room. Everyone makes it upstairs and stand behind me.

"Sweetness it's ok we can handle all this." Dean tries to calm me but I don't want to be calmed. I am so sick of this shit so I shot again this time hitting my mother in her thigh.

"You put my entire family in danger for what because I like women and men. You have that much hate in your heart for your own daughter." I shout.

"Babe we're going to be ok just put the gun down before you do something you regret." Meira tries to calm me down next.

"If you guys don't stop trying to calm me down one of you are going to catch one of these fucking bullets." I warn them and they all straighten up behind me.

"They promised us you'd all be dead and she would inherit all of your money and we would manage it all." My egg donor cries out.

"Wait you were willing to sacrifice ten fucking children all so you can get her damn inheritance but I'm the sinner. You know what fuck this." I head shot both of their asses with a heavy sigh of relief.

"Sorry about the mess Chase." I apologize once I realize their brains are splattered all over his new walls.

"Don't worry about it Suga we will get it cleaned up for him." Jax offers.

"Sweetness are you ok."

"I am now. We have about an hour and a half before they get here so we need to get the kids, our moms, and Uncle Tone to the safe house." I recite the plan we created just in case anything ever happened. Everyone finally gets the memo that I am good and start to move around cleaning up the mess.

"Family of badass women, damn y'all set the bar high well all except you." Meech compliments us then looks over to Kenya who is standing in the hall looking like she's about to throw up.

"Meechy." Meira calls in that mommy tone she does so freakishly well.

"Sorry Kenya I just don't like how you're treating my brother." He apologizes then walks down the hall to get more cleaning supplies for Monty and Jax. They continue with the clean while Meira and I go help Uncle Tone along with our moms get the into the corridors. The men built them throughout every home to all lead to this tunnel that takes us right into the bomb shelter or safe house whichever you decide to call it.

Chapter Twenty

Dean Fredericks

We have placed the heavily armed guards at all six gate entrances with them rotating patrol.

"So are we going to talk about how Suga just popped her parents in Chase's guest bedroom then proceeded to apologize for the mess like it was nothing." Meech questions as we are in our built-in armory getting strapped up.

"Bru she is starting to remind me of Meira." Monty admits.

"Your right but sexy isn't? It's like she healed from her traumas and turned into this lethal mommy bad ass." I say getting excited all over again just thinking about how for our kids our entire family anybody can get it in her eyes without hesitation.

"You're right it was sexy as fuck." Jax groans as he's loading his third weapon placing it in his boots. It really amazes me how far my sweetness has come in just a year though. She was my shy but curious little sweetness who just needed to find her voice and she finally has.

"Do you guys' think we're actually going to need all this?" Tru ask as he's checking his weapon.

"Honestly, I don't think anyone is going to make it past the gates but I prefer to be prepared then not. Ah great they're here." Monty states reads the message we all received. The ladies messaged to say they were safe in the bunker and they have their weapons ready. We all head out dressed in all black, army tested bulletproof vest strapped on, and our military rifles locked and loaded. We walk out the main house and we instantly hear the commotion at the front gate.

"Sounds like they are trying to ram the damn gate." Meech announces and he's right but we went with a steel gate around the entire damn property so basically, they'll need a tank to even get in here.

"Boss they are trying to come over the east and south gates." One of the guards comes through on comms.

"Catch a couple of them but the rest kill em,." Jax orders and as we thought they were no match for everyone we had lined up around the gates or the team that showed up from KC who were coming down the road when the ones outside the gates were attempting to retreat. The ones they caught unfortunately served to be useless information wise. They were paid in bitcoin and messaged through a dark web message board. They were able to tell us that it was only the team we killed that was sent and they had been trying to figure out a way in for a few days by flying drones over the house. It's been a couple days since they attempted attack and we were able to pass it off to the big kids as a drill in case something was to really happen. They go back to school soon and until we find out who the hell is after us I am going to be on edge. We had the front gate replaced today so that's one thing checked off my damn list.

"D relax I see those wheels turning and you're stressing yourself out. I'm fine the kids are fine and like you always do with your brothers you will find who's after us." My Sweetness assures me as she massages my shoulders and kisses my cheek then my neck.

"You keep that up woman and I'll bend you over this desk." She just grins at me when I turn to look at her and I hop out my chair to swiftly bend her over my desk positioning myself behind her. Just as I'm about to slide in her wet pussy my office door opens.

"Nigga did you forget how to knock?" I question Jax the moment he walks in and closes the door.

"Like I haven't seen you fuckin before. Hi Suga." He greets her as I slide into her.

"Ummm shit it's no reason you can still take my breath away over a year and a half later." She groans after catching her breath when I hit the back of her pussy.

"Well brother did you just stop in to see this fat ass giggle or did ya want something?" I question him as I slowly pull out then slam right back into her.

"FUCK" She shouts.

"You keep doing that I'll forget what I came here for. Oh, yea Meech and I are heading to Cali to check on the new club's construction." He finally lets me know what brings him in here.

"Wait do y'all thinks that's safe right now?" I ask stopping my movements.

"It's all good lil brother we will be back in a couple days besides one of Artemis parents are out there. We can check if it was them killing two birds one stone since I booked a meeting with his mother at her art gallery." He explains and I guess it is the best option. He stands and watches for another minute or two before finally leaving because Meech was blowing up his phone. Me and Sweetness finish up our quickie just in time for the baby monitor to alert us of our princess waking for her feeding and playtime. The family continues to way our options on who could it be for the next few days and we have started to lean towards it may just be Justin's dad. He is from old money and even though he wrote Justin off way back he was still his son. We get a message from Jax that it's definitely not Artemis's family they don't even know he's dead seems as though they are used to not hearing from him for long periods of time. They don't even know what he does, apparently the cut him off years ago for some sex scandal. We are having a family day with the kids while we await Jax and Meech's arrival. I hear a truck pull up but it sounds weird and the moment I see Meech.

"They took Jax!" Meech yells trying to run up the steps of the back porch with blood coming from his head, arm and clearly, he's hurt his leg. The kids run around the yard with their new puppies that just came this morning thankfully they are oblivious. When Meech collapses in Monty's arms my heart drops and I'm left wondering am I possibly about to lose two brother's today. I'm also wondering who the fuck am I about to kill.

To Be Continued....

Love Unconditional

Sneak Peak

Kenya Bergs

I know it's probably stupid for me to wreck my relationship over something that happened before I was even born but it's so fucking hard to get past it right now. Chase probably thinks I'm cheating on him but that couldn't be farther from the truth. I'm hoping what I am hiding isn't much worse than that because if it turns out that it is he will definitely leave and I just can't have that. I was actually thinking about telling him what's going on with me once we got back home but Meech showing up covered in blood saying Jax of all people has been taken lets me know once again my shit will have to wait. They start tending to him but then my phone rings while I am walking the kids to their grandparent's home and I answer when they all go inside.

"Yes." I greet the caller that's been causing all my problems.

"Kenya, I need you to come to me now. Make whatever excuse you need to but hurry up."

"I can't right now. There is some family shit happening right now. Maybe when things clear up." I offer up instead because I know it would look even worse to leave right now. That would probably send Meira over the edge and I will definitely be dead in her book.

"It wasn't a request Kenya, I said now." He demands and I'm not sure who the fuck he think he's talking to but it sure as fuck isn't me. I decide enough is enough so I hang up and block his number.

"So who was it this time Kenya?" Chase questions me scaring the hell out of me because I didn't even hear him walking up.

"Shit Chase don't sneak up on me like that and no one important." I answer still holding my chest and trying to catch my breath.

"It always seems to be no one important but you're always walking off to take the call or whispering. I'm getting sick of this shit Kenya." He groans getting frustrated with me again which seems to be the only emotion I invoke in him anymore but it's all my fault that I know.

"Chase, I promise it's not what you think just give me a bit more time please." I plead with him.

"You have until after we find my brother. If you're still with this bullshit you can go, I won't live in secret with the woman I vowed to love and marry one day." He puts his foot down and I almost want to tell him not but Monty comes through on our watches for him to get back to the house. He walk off without another word and now I'm hoping that however they get Jax back doesn't cause him not to make it back home.

About The Author

Lala B.

Lala B. is now three books in the game and many other stories are in the works. She is still learning all the ins and outs of the literary world and welcomes all constructive criticism to help advance her into being a great author. She loves creating stories that create a safe space for others to dream and open up their minds to new experiences. She has been writing since she was middle school age starting out with short urban stories and has even dabbled in the paranormal realm. She plans on bringing all those books to life for you all to enjoy.

You can keep in touch by following us on social media:

www.facebook.com/AuthorLaLaB

IG: Lalareadsnwrites

Bluesky: AuthorLalaB

Website: www.sipngrabyouabook.com

Books By The Author

Love Unconventional: The Fredericks Family Series Book One

I Married My Dead Cousins Husband – Novella

Love Unapologetic: The Fredericks Family Series Book Two

Upcoming Books

Love Unconditional: The Fredericks Family Series Book Three – Release date TBA

From Likes To Late Nights – Two Part Series – Released date TBA